Praise for *Arkansas*

"Leavitt is . . . the kind of writer who goes on . . . refining in book after book a select handful of themes. . . . often to spectacular result." — *Washington Post*

"Filled with interesting characters and mordant wit . . . spectacularly effective fiction." — *Time*

"Sly, self-knowing and hilarious." — *New York Times Book Review*

"Like many of the best short story collections, *Arkansas* is held together by . . . the themes of the emotions of vacancy . . . Very powerful." — *Lambda Book Report*

"Both enjoyable and scandalous. It's not just fun, its deliberately risky . . . it's a riot . . . wickedly, bitterly funny." — *Newsday*

"Leavitt's characteristic grace as a stylist and sharpness of eye is evident . . . an enticing and very well achieved collection of stories." — *Minneapolis Star Tribune*

"Exquisite, intelligent writing. Leavitt explores loneliness, longing and entitlement with careful, precise language that is a privilege to read." — *Detroit Free Press*

"The remarkable talent of a plainly first-rate writer . . . invites richly insightful observations . . . As always, Leavitt is scrupulously attentive to the enormity and complexity of sexual drives . . . The pleasure of reading his work renews itself again and again." — *Virginia Quarterly Review*

"A wonderful collection . . . some of the best David Leavitt fiction to date, typical of his ability to mine the deepest seams of human enterprise . . . Leavitt proves again his masterful handling of the moral and emotional conflicts that homosexuality presents." — *Philadelphia Inquirer*

"A wizard at blending levity and pathos, Leavitt writes gracefully about wounded, acutely self-conscious characters." — *Chicago Tribune*

ALSO BY DAVID LEAVITT

Family Dancing

The Lost Language of Cranes

Equal Affections

A Place I've Never Been

While England Sleeps

Italian Pleasures
(*with Mark Mitchell*)

Pages Passed from Hand to Hand
(*edited with Mark Mitchell*)

The Page Turner

David Leavitt

Arkansas

THREE NOVELLAS

A MARINER BOOK
Houghton Mifflin Company
BOSTON NEW YORK

Library of Congress Cataloging-in-Publication Data
Leavitt, David.
Arkansas : three novellas / David Leavitt.
p. cm.
Contents: The term paper artist — The wooden anniversary — Saturn Street.
ISBN 0-395-83704-9 ISBN 0-395-90128-6 (pbk.)
1. Gays — United States — Fiction. I. Title.
PS3562.E2618A89 1997
813'.54 — dc21 96-44315 CIP

Printed in the United States of America

QUM 10 9 8 7 6 5 4 3 2

Book design by Melodie Wertelet

A portion of "The Wooden Anniversary" originally appeared — as "Podere" — in *Italian Pleasures* (Chronicle Books, 1996).
"Milordo Inglese" from *Poems about People or England Reclaimed* by Osbert Sitwell, courtesy of David Higham Associates.
Poems by E. M. Forster, courtesy of King's College, Cambridge, and the Society of Authors as the literary representatives of the E. M. Forster Estate.

FOR

MARK MITCHELL

AUTHOR'S NOTE

For information concerning Lords Henry and Arthur Somerset, as well as Jack the Ripper, I am indebted to the following sources: *Prince Eddy and the Homosexual Underground* by Theo Aronson (John Murray, 1994), *The Cleveland Street Scandal* by H. Montgomery Hyde (W. H. Allen, 1976), *The Cleveland Street Affair* by Colin Simpson, Lewis Chester, and David Leitch (Weidenfeld and Nicolson, 1977), and *The Complete Jack the Ripper* by Donald Rumbelow (W. H. Allen, 1976).

CONTENTS

"I should like to flee
like a wounded hart
into Arkansas."

attributed to Oscar Wilde,
near the end of his life

The Term Paper Artist

I.

I WAS IN TROUBLE. An English poet (now dead) had sued me over a novel I had written because it was based in part on an episode from his life. Worse, my publishers in the United States and England had capitulated to this poet, pulling the novel out of bookstores and pulping several thousand copies.

Why should I have been surprised? My publishers were once Salman Rushdie's publishers too.

I didn't live in Los Angeles then. Instead I was on an extended visit to my father. After his retirement a few years ago, he moved down from the Bay Area to Glendale because his wife, Jean, teaches at a university not far from there. They own a newish house, rambling and ceremonial, rather like a lecture hall. This house, which originally belonged to a movie producer, includes a "media room," the electronic controls of which are so complex that even after five years, neither one has figured them out; a lighting system more various and subtle than that of most Broadway theaters; a burglar alarm they can never quite explain to Guadalupe, the cleaning lady, who seems always to be tripping it accidentally. The trouble may be that the house was built in the mid-eighties, when technology was already amazing but not yet simple. And because technology, like money, is measured by our needs — had she lived in our age, George Eliot might have said that — most of this gadgetry, by the turn of the decade, was obsolete. These days machines, like clothes, seem to lose their value merely with the passing of seasons.

In any event, it was to my father, and his complicated house, that I had come that fall. I had come because I couldn't write in my own house, and also because I was dating an actor: an actor who, as it happened, had gotten a part in a movie almost as soon as I'd arrived, then flown off to spend six weeks in the Andes. And as I was inclined neither to visit him in the Andes, nor to return to New York, where I had fallen into bad habits, I settled down into the life of my father's guest room, which is a pleasant, lethargic one except in one detail: because New York wakes up three hours earlier than California, when I got out of bed in the mornings, it was invariably to find faxes of a not very pleasant nature lying outside the door to my room. And this particular morning — the morning of the day I would meet Eric — the fax that lay outside the door to my room was particularly unpleasant. My American publisher, it told me, had decided to suspend publication of the paperback edition of my novel; in spite of the revisions I had made over the summer, in spite of the book already having been announced in the catalogue, "counsel" had decreed it still too dangerous to print.

There was a bad smell in the room, mossy and rotten, as if the fax itself gave off noxious vapors.

I mentioned nothing to my father except the smell. As a rule, I was trying to learn to take blows better, or at least to take them without letting them distort the natural progress of my days. So as usual I had my morning coffee at the local Starbucks. Then I drove around for a while, listening to Dr. Delia, the radio shrink. Then I tried out the computerized massage chair on display at the Sharper Image in the Beverly Center, and then I stopped in at Book Soup on Sunset to thumb through the latest issues of *The New Yorker, The New York Review of Books,* and *The New York Times Book Review,* as well as whatever books happened to have landed that morning on the "new arrivals" table. You see, it was terribly important to me in those days to stay abreast of what my *confrères* in the writing trade were up to. Competitiveness, not to mention a terror of losing the stature I had gained in my early youth, played a much more singular role in my life than I have heretofore admitted. Indeed, I suspect it plays a more singular role in most writers' lives than they are willing to admit. And the level of success makes no difference. The young poet cringing to learn that his enemy has been awarded the Guggenheim for which he has been turned down is merely a miniature version of the hugely famous novelist cringing to learn that her university colleague has won the Nobel Prize for which she has shamelessly campaigned: we are speaking, here, of the emotions of vacancy, which scale neither enhances nor mitigates; for panic and emptiness (the words are Forster's) always feel like panic and emptiness, no matter the degree.

After Book Soup, I ate lunch alone at the Mandarette Café on Beverly, then drove over to the UCLA library to research the new novel I was working on, which concerned the aftermath of the Cleveland Street Affair. This was a scandal that took place in London in the years immediately preceding the Oscar Wilde trials. Essentially, in 1889 Her Majesty's police had stumbled upon a homosexual brothel at 19 Cleveland

Street, the clients of which included Lord Arthur Somerset, a major in the Royal Horse Guards and equerry to the prince of Wales, whose stables he supervised. Telegraph boys — one of whom had the astounding name of Charles E. Thickbroom — provided the "entertainment" at this brothel, as well as most of the evidence against Lord Somerset.

My idea was to merge his story with that of his brother, Lord *Henry* Somerset, who had fled England for Florence ten years earlier after his wife had caught him *in flagrante delicto* with a boy called Henry Smith. (Lady Somerset would later become a famous temperance advocate.) History has tended to confuse, even to fuse, the brothers, and I was following history's lead.

So there I sat, in a carrel in the stacks of the UCLA library, with an open legal pad and a pile of books in front of me, doing, if truth be told, very little. Partially this was because by nature I am not a researcher. I grow impatient with facts. And yet I cannot deny the more pressing reason for my indolence: it was fear. An aureole of worried expectancy seemed to surround the prospect of this next novel. I thought I could hear it in the voice of my agent, my editor, even my father. Would I ever be allowed to forget what had happened with *While England Sleeps*? I wondered. Or would the scandal that had attached itself to the novel's publication — to quote a helpful journalist — "taint my aura" forever? I couldn't yet say.

Thus my UCLA afternoon, like all my UCLA afternoons, proceeded. Instead of studying the "blackmailer's charter," which in England criminalized "acts of gross indecency between adult men in public or private," I got a Diet Coke from a vending machine. Instead of reading up on the Italian Penal Code of 1889, by virtue of which Italy became such a mecca for homosexual émigrés, I martyred myself to *Publishers Weekly*.

Instead of investigating Florence's amazingly casual attitude toward sodomy, I investigated whether anyone sexy was loitering in the photocopy area. Finally around three, having devoted at best a paltry hour to the skimming of history books and the jotting down of notes, I left. Impending traffic on the 210 was my excuse. And yet somehow I managed, as always, to find time for a visit to the Circus of Books on Santa Monica Boulevard, where I wasted just enough minutes browsing at the porn magazines to ensure getting stuck in the same rush hour traffic I'd departed the library early to avoid. It was six-thirty by the time I pulled into my father's driveway.

Feeling rather cross, I got out of the car and went inside. Three people I didn't know were drinking iced tea in the living room. They looked at me. I looked at them. "Hello," we all said, and then Jean and my father — one bearing a platter of raw vegetables, the other a bowl of mushroom pâté — emerged through the swinging door from the kitchen. "Oh, hi, David!" Jean called cheerfully, and introduced me.

The three people, all of whom stood, turned out to be Cynthia Steinberg, a sociology professor at Rutgers and a colleague from Jean's graduate school days; her husband, Jack; and their son Eric. Eric, I quickly learned, was an economics major at UCLA who hoped to attend Stanford Business School; and as my father has taught for several decades at that august institution, this little drinks party had been arranged so that Eric could ask questions, get advice, and perhaps (this is my conjecture; it was never stated) ingratiate my father into writing him a letter of recommendation.

Now, it has actually become quite a common occurrence for old friends of my father's and Jean's to bring their children over for academic advice. And probably because I was so used to the well-heeled, eager-eyed boys and girls I tended to encounter, all of them hell-bent on making an executive impression, Eric surprised me. For one thing, he had large, placid blue eyes with which, as I accepted Jean's proffered glass of tea, he stared at me: a stare that had no caution in it. Eric wasn't exactly handsome; his nose obtruded, and he had thick, stupid lips — the best for kissing. Still, imperfect features can fit together with a mysterious harmony that is altogether more alluring than beauty. And it was this somewhat cobbled-together aspect of his appearance that attracted me: his long legs in khaki pants, which he could not keep still; his brown loafers, above the scuffed edges of which, when he slung one leg over the other, a tanned and hairy ankle was exposed; his too-short tie and brown jacket; and the hair that fell into his eyes: yes, I am back at his eyes; I always end up back at his eyes. For what took me off guard, as I sat across from him (Jean was talking about GMATs), was their frankness. They were like the eyes of children who are too young to have learned that it is not nice to peer. And Eric did peer; at me, at my father, at the garden through the plate-glass windows. His mother asked all his questions for him. He only nodded occasionally, or muttered a monosyllable.

It took me ten minutes before I realized how stoned he was.

Eventually talk of business schools dried up. "So are you living in L.A. now, David?" Eric's father asked.

"Just visiting," I said.

"David lives in New York," my father said brightly. "He's out here working on his new book."

"Oh, you're a writer?" This was Eric speaking — the first question he'd asked since I'd arrived.

"When I'm able to work," I said, "I call myself a writer."

"David's done very well for himself," Mrs. Steinberg informed Eric. "You know I wasn't going to say anything — I figure you must hear it all the time — but I really loved *Family Dancing.*"

"Thanks. Actually, I don't hear it all the time."

"What do you write?" Eric asked.

"Novels, short stories," I said, and braced myself for the question that would inevitably follow: *What kind of novels? What kind of short stories?* But Eric only smiled. His teeth were very large.

"And you make a living at it?"

"Usually."

"What did you major in?"

"English."

"Great. Where'd you go to school?"

"Yale."

"Cool. My teacher — I'm taking this English lit class? My teacher went to Yale. Her name's Mary Yearwood. She's probably about your age."

"I don't know her."

"She's an expert on Henry James. Did you go to grad school?"

"No. I pretty much started publishing out of college."

"I'd really like to read some of your books. Maybe you could tell me the titles."

"Well, we'd better be going," Mrs. Steinberg said, rising very suddenly from the sofa. "We've kept you folks long enough."

"No, no." My father did not sound very convincing, however, and soon the Steinbergs were moving toward the door, where farewells were exchanged. Meanwhile I hurried into the kitchen and wrote the titles of my books on a memo pad advertising Librax.

"Thanks," Eric said, as I handed him the list. "I'll definitely pick one up." And he held out his hand.

We shook. His handshake was — everything about Eric was — long, loose, generous.

They left.

"A nice kid," my father said.

"Very nice," Jean agreed. "Still, Cynthia's worried. Apparently he's a whiz with computers — but not exactly verbal."

"C's in English won't get him into Stanford," my father said. (We had all strolled into the kitchen.)

"What does English matter if you want to go to business school?" I asked.

"It didn't used to. But then there were always too many technicians, and so what we're looking for now are all-around students with a good background in the humanities. You, for instance, my boy" — he put a hand on my shoulder — "would probably have had an easier time getting into Stanford than Eric Steinberg will."

"But I didn't want to."

"I still wish you'd applied. You could have been the first student in the school's history to get a simultaneous MFA and MBA —"

"Yes, I know, Dad."

Jean went up to her study while my father took some yellow beets from the freezer and put them in a microwavable dish.

"By the way, do you still have that stink in your room?" he asked.

"Yes," I said. "It's the strangest thing. I started noticing it after the tremor."

"Tremor! What tremor?" He walked over to the intercom. "Jean, did you feel a tremor?" he shouted.

"No, I didn't!" she shouted back. For some reason they always yelled at each other through the intercom, as if they didn't quite trust it to carry their voices.

After that I changed my routine. Instead of wasting my mornings on the road, I went directly from Starbucks to the library, and stayed there until lunch.

I wish I could say I got a little more work done over the course of those days than I might have otherwise, but I didn't. Instead I spent most of my time looking up various literary acquaintances in the periodicals index to see how much more work they had published in the previous year than I had; or chasing down those bad reviews of *While England Sleeps* that my publisher had had the good sense not to forward to me (the worst of these, in *The Partisan Review*, was by one Pearl K. Bell, whose son had been my classmate); or reading and rereading the terrible press I'd gotten during the lawsuit. Also, I looked every day to see if anyone (Eric?) might have checked out any of my books. (No one had; I took the occasion to autograph them.) After which I'd lunch, drive around, and end up more often than not (no, I am lying: every day) at the Circus of Books.

Coming home one evening, I walked through my father's door only to hear Jean shouting through the intercom that I had a phone call.

"It's Eric," Eric said when I picked up. Not "Eric Steinberg," just "Eric" — as if he took it for granted that I'd remember him.

"Eric, how're you doing?"

"All right, yourself?"

"Great."

"Cool."

There was a silence. Naturally I presumed that since Eric had called me, he would also shoulder the responsibility for keeping the conversation going. He didn't.

It soon became apparent that if I didn't say something, no one would.

"So what are you up to?"

"Oh, you know, the usual. Studying. Partying." Another silence. "So I bought one of your books."

"Really. Which one?"

"*The Secret Language of the Cranes.*"

"Oh, right."

"Yeah."

Long pause.

"And did you like it?"

"Yeah, I thought it was pretty cool. I mean, to write all that! It takes me an hour to write a sentence."

"It's just a matter of practice," I said. "Like sports. Are you an athlete?"

"Not really."

"I was just asking because you looked to be in pretty good shape."

"I swim three times a week."

"At UCLA?"

"Uh-huh."

"Is there a good pool?"

"Pretty good. Olympic size."

More silence.

"Well, I appreciate your calling, Eric," I said. "And buying the book. Most people who say they're going to never bother."

"That's okay. I don't read much generally, but I thought your book was pretty interesting. I mean, it showed me a lot of things I didn't know, not being gay myself."

"I'm glad to hear you say that," I said in one breath, "because sometimes I think gay writers only write for a gay audience, which is a mistake. The point is, human experience is universal, and there's no reason why straight people can't get as much out of a gay novel as gay people get out of a straight novel, don't you think?" (I grimaced: I sounded as if I were giving an interview.)

"Yeah" was Eric's reply.

A fifth, nearly unbearable silence.

"Well, it's been great talking to you, Eric."

"My pleasure."

"Okay, so long."

"Later."

And he hung up with amazing swiftness.

The next morning I was at the library when it opened.

I stayed all day. Did you know that Lord Henry Somerset's father, the Duke of Beaufort, invented the game of badminton, which was named for his estate? Well, he did. Also, Osbert Sitwell once wrote a poem about Lord Henry, in which he lampooned the notorious expatriate as "Lord Richard Vermont," whom "some nebulous but familiar scandal / Had lightly blown . . . over the Channel, / Which he never crossed again."

> Thus at the age of twenty-seven
> A promising career was over,
> And the thirty or forty years that had elapsed
> Had been spent in killing time

— or so Lord Richard thought,
Though in reality, *killing time*
Is only the name for another of the multifarious ways
By which Time kills us.

When I got home that evening, there was a message in my room that Eric had called.

"Hey," I said, calling him back, calmer now, as well as more curious.

"Hey," Eric said.

Apparently it was not his conversational style to phone for any particular reason.

"So what's up?"

"Not much, man. Just kicking back."

"Sounds good. You live in a dorm?"

"No, I'm off campus."

"Oh, cool." (Lying down, I shoved a pillow behind my head, as I imagined Eric had.) "And do you live alone?"

"I share a house with two other guys, but I've got my own room." He yawned.

"And are your roommates home?"

"Nope. They're at the library."

"Studying?"

"You got it."

"And don't you have studying to do?"

"Yeah, but I bagged it around seven. Actually, I was feeling kind of bored, so I started reading another one of your books."

"Oh really? Which one?" (How I longed to ask what he was wearing!)

"*Family Dancing.* And you know what's weird? It really reminds me of my family — especially the one called 'Danny in Transit.' I'm from New Jersey," he added.

"Wow," I said. *Family Dancing* was the last thing I wanted to talk about it. "So what do you do with your spare time, Eric? Besides swim three days a week."

"You've got a good memory, Dave."

"Thanks. It goes with the territory."

"Like that story of yours! So let's see, what do I do with my spare time." (I heard him thinking.) "You mean besides jack off?"

"Well —"

Eric laughed. "Let's see. Well, I like to party sometimes —"

"I'm sorry to interrupt, but I have to ask — when you say party, do you mean literally party, or get high?"

"Can be both, can be both."

"You were stoned at my father's house the other day, weren't you?"

"Shit! How'd you know?"

"I could just tell."

"Do you get high?"

"Sometimes."

"Man, I am so into pot! Ever since I was thirteen. Listen, do you want to come over and get stoned?"

I sat up. "Sure," I said.

"Cool."

Long pause.

"Wait — you mean tonight?"

"Yeah, why not?"

"No problem, tonight's fine. I just don't want to keep you from your studying."

"I told you, I bagged it."

"Okay. Where do you live?"

"Santa Monica. Have you got a pencil?"

I wrote down the directions.

Through the intercom, I told Jean I was going out to a movie with my friend Gary, after which I got into the car and headed for the freeway. The rush hour traffic had eased, which meant it took me only half an hour to arrive at the address Eric had given me, a dilapidated clapboard house. In the dark I couldn't make out the color.

From the salty flavor of the air, I could tell that the sea wasn't far off.

Dogs barked as I got out of my father's car and opened the peeling picket gate, over which unpruned hydrangea bushes crowded. The planks of the verandah creaked as I stepped across them. In the windows, a pale orange light quavered.

I knocked. Somewhere in the distance Tracy Chapman was singing "Fast Car."

"Hey, sexy," Eric said, pulling open the screen door.

I blinked. He was wearing sweatpants and a Rutgers Crew T-shirt.

"Glad you could make it." He held the door open.

"My pleasure," I said.

I stepped inside. The living room, with its orange carpet and beaten-up, homely furniture, reminded me of my own student days, when I'd shopped at the Salvation Army, or dragged armchairs in from the street.

"Nice place," I said.

"It's home," Eric said. "I mean, it's not like your dad's house. Now *that's* what I call a house. Say, you want a beer?"

"Sure." I wasn't about to tell him I hated beer.

He brought two Coronas from the kitchen, one of which he handed me.

"*L'chaim,*" he toasted.

"Cheers," I said.

Then Eric leapt up the staircase, and since he gave no indication whether or not I was supposed to follow him, I followed him. He took the stairs three at a time.

At the top, four doors opened off a narrow corridor. Only one was ajar.

"Step into my office," he said, passing through. "And close the door behind you."

I did. The room was shadowy. An architect's lamp with a long, folding arm illuminated a double mattress on the floor, the blue sheets clumped at the bottom. Against the far wall, under a window, stood a desk piled with textbooks. Clean white socks were heaped on a chair, beneath which lounged a pair of crumpled jockey shorts.

In the space where a side table might have been, a copy of *Family Dancing* lay splayed over the Vintage edition of *A Room with a View*.

"Have a seat," Eric said. Then he threw himself onto the mattress, where, cross-legged, he busied himself with a plastic bag of pot and some rolling papers.

"You can move all that," he added, indicating the chair.

Gingerly I put the socks onto the desk, nudged the shorts with my left foot, and sat down.

Unspeaking, with fastidious concentration, Eric rolled the joint. Much about his room, from the guitar to the recharging laptop to the blue-lit CD player (the source of Tracy Chapman's voice), seemed to me typical UCLA. And yet there were incongruous touches. For one thing, the posters did not depict acid rock musicians or figures from the world of sports. Instead Eric had thumbtacked the Sistine Chapel ceiling onto his ceiling. Over his bed hung the *Last Judgment.* Caspar David Friedrich's *Wanderer in a Sea of Mist* stared into the back of the door.

"Have you spent much time in Europe?" I hazarded.

"Yeah, last summer. I went to Italy, France, Amsterdam."

"You must have liked Amsterdam."

"I basically don't remember Amsterdam."

I laughed. "And Italy?"

"Man! Rome was amazing! Rome really blew me away!" Licking the joint, he sealed it, then picked up a lighter from the floor.

"The last time I went to Florence I tried to find the hotel where Forster stayed," I said. "I only mention it because I see you're reading *A Room with a View*."

Eric lit the joint. "Come on down here," he said, slapping the other side of the bed like someone's behind.

"I'd better take off my shoes."

"Yeah, Dave, I'd have to agree that would be a good idea."

He was mocking me, but agreeably, and, flushing, I did what I was told. Down among the sheets the world smelled both fruity and smoky.

Eric toked, passed me the joint. Lying back, he stretched his arms over his head.

"*Two weeks in a Virginia jail,*" Tracy Chapman sang, "*for my lover, for my lover.*" And on the next line, Eric joined in: "*Twenty-thousand-dollar bail, for my lover, for my lover* . . ."

"You've got a nice voice," I said when he'd finished the song.

"Thanks."

"Me, I'm tone-deaf. I get it from my dad."

"Your dad seems like a decent guy."

"He is. I liked your parents too. Have they left yet, by the way?"

"Finally." He breathed out bitter fumes. "I mean, my parents, they're nice and all, but after a few days — you know what I mean?"

"Sure."

Propping myself on one elbow, I looked at him. His eyes were getting red. In silence, I watched the way his swollen lips seemed to narrow around the joint, like some strange species of fish; the way his stomach distended and relaxed, distended and relaxed; the meshing of his lashes, when he closed his eyes.

"This is good pot," I said after a while.

Eric had his feet crossed at the ankles. From beneath his T-shirt's hem, the drawstring of his sweatpants peeked out like a little noose.

I forget what we talked about next. Maybe Michelangelo. Conversation blurred and became inchoate, and only sharpened again when Eric looked at me, and said, "So do you want to give me a blow job?"

I opened my eyes as wide as my stoned state permitted. "A blow job?"

"Yeah. Like in your book. You know, when Eliot's sitting at his desk and Philip sucks him off."

"Oh, you remember that scene."

"Yeah."

"And what makes you think I'd want to give you a blow job?"

"Well, the way I see it, you're gay and I'm sexy. So why not?"

"But you have to want it, too. Do you?"

"Sure."

"How much? A lot?"

"Enough."

"Are you hard now?"

"Yeah, I guess."

"You guess?"

I reached over and grabbed his crotch. "Yeah, I guess so too."

"Well, go ahead." Eric crossed his arms behind his head.

Untying the little noose of the drawstring, I pulled back his sweatpants and underwear. Like his handshake, his cock was long and silky. It rested upon a pile of lustrous black pubic hair rather like a sausage on top of a plate of black beans: I apologize for this odd culinary metaphor, but it was what entered my mind at the time. And Eric was laughing.

"What's so funny?"

"Nothing, it's just that . . . you're really gay, aren't you?"

"Is that a surprise?"

"No, no. I'm just . . . I mean, you're really into my dick, aren't you? This is so wild!"

"What's wild about it?"

"Because it's like, here you are, really into my dick, whereas probably if you saw, you know, a vagina or something, you'd be sort of disgusted, or not interested. But if you showed me your dick, I'd be like, I could care less."

"You want me to show you my dick?"

"Not really."

"You want me to give you a really great blow job, Eric?"

"Actually, I had something else in mind."

All at once he leapt off the mattress. I sat up. Putting his cock away, he started rummaging through the mess on his desk.

"Here it is," he said after a minute, and threw a copy of *Daisy Miller* at me.

"*Daisy Miller*?"

"Have you read it?"

"Of course."

"I have to do this paper on it. It's due next Tuesday." He read aloud from a photocopy on the desk: "'Compare and contrast Lucy's and Daisy's responses to Italy in Forster's *A Room with a View* and James's *Daisy Miller.*' This is for Professor Yearwood," he added.

"Uh-huh."

"And I've really got to ace this paper because I got a C on the midterm. It wasn't that I didn't do the reading. I'm not one of those guys who just reads the Cliffs Notes or anything. The problem was the essay questions. What can I tell you, Dave? I've got great ideas, but I can't write to save my ass."

He lay down on the mattress again and started flipping through *Daisy Miller.* "So last year my friend bought a paper from this company, Intellectual Properties Inc. They sell papers for $79.95, and they've got, like, thousands on file. And my friend bought one and got caught. He ended up being expelled." Eric rubbed his nose. "I can't risk that. Still, I need to ace the paper. That's where you come in."

"Where I come in?"

"Exactly. You can write my paper for me. And if I get a good grade, you can give me a blow job." He winked.

"Wait a minute," I said.

Eric reached for, and switched on, his laptop. "Actually I've already started taking notes. Maybe you can use them."

"Hold on! Stop."

He stopped.

"You don't honestly think I'm going to write your paper for you, do you?"

"Why not?"

"Well, I mean, Eric, I'm a famous writer. I have a novel under contract with Viking Penguin. You know, Viking Penguin, that gigantic publisher, the same one that published *Daisy Miller*? And they're paying me a lot of money — *a lot* of money — to write this novel. On top of which what you're proposing — it's unethical. It goes against everything I believe in."

"Yeah, if I were asking you to make up the ideas! But I'm not. You can use *my* ideas. I'm just asking you to put the sentences together." He stubbed out the joint. "Shit, you're a really great writer, Dave. I'll bet you never got less than an A on a paper in your life, did you? Did you?"

"No."

"Exactly." He brushed an eyelash off my cheek. "So the way I see it is this. I've got something you want. You've got something I need. We make a deal. I mean, your dad teaches at Stanford Business School. Hasn't he taught you anything? Now here are my notes."

He thrust the laptop at me. Words congealed on the gray screen.

I read.

"Well?" Eric said after a few minutes.

"First of all, you're wrong about Daisy. She's not nearly so knowing as you make out."

"How so?"

"It's the whole point. She's actually very innocent, maybe the most innocent character in the story."

"Yeah, according to Winterbourne. I don't buy it. I've known girls like that, they only act innocent when the shit hits the fan. Otherwise —"

"But that's a very narrow definition of innocence. Innocence can also mean unawareness that what other people think matters."

"I see your point."

"Oh, and I like what you say about George being part of the Italian landscape. That's very astute."

"Really? See, I was thinking about that scene with the violets — how he's, like, one with the violets."

"Which book did you enjoy more?"

"*A Room with a View,* definitely."

"Me too. I don't — what I should say is, I'll always admire James. But I'll never love him. He's too — I don't know. Fussy. Also, he never gets under Italy's skin, which is odd, because Forster does, and he spent so much less time there."

"The paper's supposed to be ten to fifteen pages," Eric said. "I need it Tuesday A.M."

"I haven't said yes."

"Are you saying no?"

"I'm saying I have to think about it."

"Well, think fast, because Professor Yearwood deducts half a grade for every day a paper's overdue. She's a ballbreaker."

"And what'll you do if I do say no?"

"You won't say no, Dave. I know you won't because I'm your friend, and you're not the kind of guy who lets down a friend in need."

It seemed natural, at this point, to get up off the bed and head downstairs, where Eric put a paternal arm around my shoulder. "Dave," he said. "Dave, Dave, Dave. Dave, Dave, Dave, Dave, Dave."

"By the way," I said, "you do realize that both Forster and James were gay."

"No shit. Still, it makes sense. The way they seem to understand the girls' point of view and all." He opened the creaking screen door. "So when do I hear from you?"

"Tomorrow." I stepped out onto the verandah.

"It'll have to be tomorrow," Eric said, "because if you don't write this paper for me, I've got to figure out some alternative plan. And if you do —" Pulling down his sweatpants, he flashed his cock, which was hard again — if it had ever gotten soft.

"How old are you, by the way?"

"Twenty last month. Why?"

"Just wondering."

He reached out a hand, but instead I shook his cock. "Whoa, no way!" Eric said, laughing as he backed off. "For that you have to wait till Tuesday."

"Only kidding," I said.

"Later," Eric said, closing the door, after which I headed back out into the salty night.

"Society garlic," Jean said the next morning.

"What?"

"That smell in your bedroom. It was the flowers. They're called society garlic because they're pretty but they stink. And Guadalupe picked them and put them in your bedroom. You remember she took that ikebana course?" Jean sighed loudly. "Anyway, we're airing the room out now."

"Guadalupe didn't realize it at the time," my father said. "She just thought they were normal flowers."

Jean poured some cold tea into a mug and put it in the microwave. In the wake of last night's adventures, I'd completely forgotten about the odor in my bedroom, which had apparently troubled my father to a considerable degree. "Yesterday while you were at the library I must have spent an hour and a half going through your room," he said. "Top to bottom, and I still couldn't figure out where the smell was coming from. Toward the end I was worried something had crawled into the wall and died."

"What movie did you see last night?" Jean asked.

"Oh, we didn't end up going to a movie. We just had coffee."

"Gary's a nice fellow."

"I forgot to tell you," my father said. "That other friend of yours phoned last night. Andy, is that his name? And he says he's in the Andes." He laughed.

"I know. He's making a movie."

"He left a number. I'm not sure what the time difference is, but I can check."

"Don't worry. I can't call him back now anyway. I've got to get to the library."

"You certainly seem to be working hard these days," Jean said. Then she took her cup of tea up to her study. My father started the *Times* crossword puzzle. "Younger son of a Spanish monarch," he read aloud. "Seven letters."

"*Infante,*" I said. Needless to say, it worried me to imagine him searching my room top to bottom: had he discovered the stash of pornography in the dresser drawer?

After that I left for the library. You will notice that in my account of these weeks I have not made a single reference to the act of writing, even though it is the ostensible source of my income and reputation. Well, the sad truth was, for close to a year, my entire literary output had consisted of one book review and two pages of a short story (abandoned). Research was my excuse, yet I wasn't really interested in my research either, and so when I got to the library that morning I bypassed the 1890s altogether, opting instead for a battered copy of Furbank's biography of Forster. According to Furbank, Forster met James only once, when he was in his late twenties. The master, "rather fat but fine, and effectively bald," confused him with G. E. Moore, while "the beautiful Mrs. von Glehn" served tea. Yet even as Forster felt "all that the ordinary healthy man feels in the presence of a lord," James moved him less than the young laborer he encountered on the way home from Lamb House, smoking and leaning against a wall. Of this laborer, he wrote in a poem,

> No youthful flesh weighs down your youth.
> You are eternal, infinite,
> You are the unknown, and the truth.

And he also wrote,

> For those within the room, high talk,
> Subtle experience — for me
> That spark, that darkness, on the walk.

Poor Forster! I thought. He'd never had an easy time of it; had passed his most virile years staring at handsome youths from a needful distance while his mother dragged him in the opposite direction. Rooms "where culture unto culture knelt" beckoned him, but something else beckoned him as well, and the call of that something — "that spark, that darkness, on the walk" — he hadn't been able to answer until late in his life. No, I decided, he wouldn't have warmed much to James, that conscientious objector in the wars of sexuality, exempted from battle by virtue of his "obscure hurt." (How coy, how typically Jamesian, that phrase!) Whereas Forster, dear Forster, was in his own way the frankest of men. Midway through his life, in a New Year's assessment, he wrote, "The anus is clotted with hairs, and there is a great loss of sexual power — it was very violent 1920–22." He gathered signatures in support of Radclyffe Hall when *The Well of Loneliness* was banned, while James distanced himself from Oscar Wilde during his trials, fearful lest the association should taint. And this seems natural: fear, in the Jamesian universe, seems natural. Whereas Forster would have betrayed his country before he betrayed his friend.

I closed the Furbank. I was trying to remember the last time a boy had inspired me to write a poem. Ages, I realized; a decade. And now, out of the blue, here was Eric, neither beautiful nor wise, physically indifferent to me, yet capable of a crude, affectionate sincerity that cut straight through reason to strum the very fibers of my poetry-making aeolian heart. *Oh, Eric!* I wanted to sing. *Last night I was happy. I'd forgotten what it was like to be happy. Because for years, it has just been anxiety and antidotes to anxiety, numbing consolations that look like happiness but exist only to bandage, to assuage; whereas happiness is never merely a bandage; happiness is newborn every time, impulsive and fledgling every time. Happiness, yes! As if a shoot, newly uncurled, were moving in growth toward the light of your pale eyes!*

I got up from where I was sitting. I walked to the nearest pay phone and called him.

"Hello?" he said groggily.

"Did I wake you?"

"No problem." A loud yawn. "What time is it anyway? Shit, eleven." A sound of nose-blowing. "So what's the word, Dave?"

"I've decided to do it."

"Great."

"You need the paper Tuesday, right? Well, what say I come by your place Monday night?"

"Not here. My roommate's sister's visiting."

"Okay. Then how about we meet somewhere else?"

"As long as it's off campus."

I suggested the Ivy, a gay coffee bar in West Hollywood that Eric had never heard of, and he agreed.

"Till Monday, then."

"Later."

He hung up.

I went back to my carrel. I gathered up all the 1890s research books I'd kept on hold and dumped them in the return bin. (They fell to the bottom with a gratifying thunk.) Then I went into the literature stacks and pulled out some appealingly threadbare editions of *A Room with a View* and *Daisy Miller,* which I spent the afternoon rereading. Believe me or not as you choose: only four times did I get up: once for a candy bar, once for lunch, twice to go to the bathroom. And what a surprise! These books, which I hadn't looked at for years, steadied and deepened the happiness Eric had flamed in me. It had been too long, I realized, since I'd read a novel that wasn't by one of my contemporaries, a novel that smelled old. Now, sitting in that library near a window through which the fall sun occasionally winked, a naive pleasure in reading reawoke in me. I smiled when Miss Bartlett was unequal to the bath. I smiled when the Reverend Beebe threw off his clothes and dived into the sacred lake. And when Randolph Miller said, "You bet," and the knowing Winterbourne "reflected on that depth of Italian subtlety, so strangely opposed to Anglo-Saxon simplicity, which enables people to show a smoother surface in proportion as they're more acutely displeased." That was good.

That was James at his best. *Oh, literature, literature!* — I was singing again — *it was toward your pantheon that fifteen years ago, for the first time, I inclined my reading eyes: not the world of lawsuits and paperback floors, the buzz and the boom and the bomb; no, it was this joy I craved, potent as the fruity perfume of a twenty-year-old boy's unwashed sheets.*

That afternoon — again, you can believe me or not, as you choose — I read until dinnertime.

"Dad, are you using your computer?" I asked when I got home.

"Not tonight."

"Mind if I do?"

From his crossword puzzle he looked up at me, a bit surprised if truth be told, for it had been many weeks since I'd made such a request.

"Help yourself," he said. "There should be paper in the printer."

"Thanks." And going into his study, I switched on the machine, so that within a few seconds that all too familiar simulacrum of the blank page was confronting me.

Very swiftly — blankness can be frightening — I typed:

"That Spark, That Darkness on the Walk":
Responses to Italy in *Daisy Miller* and *A Room with a View*
by Eric Steinberg

After which I leaned back and looked admiringly at my title.

Good, I thought, now to begin writing. And did.

I dressed up for my meeting with Eric at the Ivy that Monday. First I got a haircut; then I bathed and shaved; then I put on a new beige vest I'd bought at Banana Republic, a white Calvin

Klein shirt, and fresh jeans. And at the risk of sounding immodest, I must say that the effect worked: I looked good, waiting for him in that little oasis of homosexual civility with my cappuccino and my copy of *Where Angels Fear to Tread.* Except that it hardly mattered. Eric arrived late, and only stayed five minutes. His eyes were glazed, his hair unwashed, his green down vest gave off a muddy smell, as if it had been left out in the rain.

"Man, I feel like shit" was his greeting as he sat down.

"What's the matter?"

"I haven't slept in three nights. I've got this huge econ project due Wednesday. Airline deregulation."

"You want some coffee?"

"I have had so much coffee in the last twenty-four hours!" He rubbed his eyes.

We were silent for a few seconds. Waiting, I'd been curious to know what he'd make of the Ivy, the clientele of whom consisted pretty exclusively of West Hollywood homos. Now I saw that he wasn't awake enough to notice.

"So do you have it?" he asked presently.

"Yeah, I have it." Reaching into my briefcase, I handed him the paper. "Seventeen pages, footnoted and typed in perfect accordance with MLA style rules."

Eric thumbed through the sheets. "Great," he said, scanning. "Yeah, this is just the sort of shit Professor Yearwood'll eat up."

Stuffing the paper into his backpack, he stood.

"Well, thanks, Dave. Gotta run."

"Already?"

"Like I said, I've got this econ project due."

"But I thought . . . "

My voice trailed off into silence.

"Oh, that," Eric said, smiling. "*After* I get my grade. I mean, what if she gives me a D?" He winked. "Oh, and *after* I'm done with fucking airline deregulation. Well, later."

He was gone.

Rather despondently, I finished my cappuccino.

Well, you've learned your lesson, a voice inside me said. Ripped off again. And not only that, you can never tell anyone. It would be too embarrassing.

I know, I know.

Alas, it was not the first time this voice had given me such a lecture.

I drove home. My father and Jean were out. Locking myself in the guest room, I took off my Banana Republic vest, my Calvin Klein shirt, my no longer fresh jeans. Then I got into bed and called the phone sex line, a particularly desperate form of consolation, to which I had not resorted for several weeks. And as is usual in that eyeless world (Andy calls it "Gaza"), various men were putting each other through panting, frenetic paces on which I couldn't concentrate; no, I couldn't concentrate on "the bunkhouse" by which one caller was obsessed, or the massage scenario another seemed intent on reenacting. Finally, feeling heartbroken and a little peevish, I hung up on Jim from Silverlake in the middle of his orgasm, after which I lay in bed with the lights on, staring at the vase from which the society garlic had been emptied; the phone, smug on its perch, coy as a cat, not ringing; of course it wasn't ringing. For Eric had his paper, and so there was no reason he would call me tonight or tomorrow night or ever. Nor would I chase him down. Like Mary Haines in *The Women,* I had my pride. He'd get his A. And probably it was better that way, since after all, the terms of the arrangement were that he would let me suck him off once, and if I sucked him off once, I'd probably want to suck him off twice; and then I'd want him to do it to me, which he wouldn't. Falling in love with straight boys — it's the tiredest of homosexual clichés; in addition to which Los Angeles circa 1994 was a far cry from Florence circa 1894, from that quaint Italian world to which Lord Henry Somerset had decamped after his divorce, that world in which almost any boy that caught your eye could be had, joyously, for a few *lire*, and without fear of blackmail or arrest. And though they would eventually marry and father children, those boys, at least they had that quaint old Italian openness to pleasure. I'd thought Eric had it too. But now I saw that more likely, he viewed his body as something to be transacted. He knew what a paper was worth — and he knew what *he* was worth; what his freshness and frankness were worth, when compared with some limp piece of faggot cock from the Circus of Books; some tired-out, overworked piece of dick; the bitter flavor of latex. (Do I cause offense? I won't apologize; it was what I felt.)

And in the morning, I did not go to the library at all. Made not even the slightest pretense of behaving like a writer. Instead I spent the whole day wandering the city. (The low business in which I got myself involved need not be catalogued here.)

Likewise the next day. And the next.

Then Eric called me.

At first, glancing at the Librax pad, I didn't quite believe it. I thought perhaps it was another Eric — except that I recognized his number.

"Dave, my man!" he said when I phoned him back. "You have got the Midas touch!"

"What?"

"An A, man! A fucking A! And an A– on my econ project!" I heard him inhale.

"That's great, Eric. Congratulations."

"Thanks. So now that you've done your part, I'm ready to do mine."

"Oh?"

"What, you're surprised?"

"Well —"

"Dave, I'm disappointed in you! I mean, do you really think I'm the kind of guy who'd let you write his paper and then just, you know, blow you off?"

"No, of course not —"

"On the contrary. You're the one who's going to do the blowing. You just tell me when, man."

I blushed. "Well, tonight would be okay."

"Both roommates away for the weekend. Plus I've got some great pot. I bought it to celebrate."

"Fantastic. So — I'll come over."

"Cool. See you in a few." He hung up.

Feeling a little shaky, I took a shower and changed my clothes. By now the beige vest from Banana Republic had gotten stretched out, and the Calvin Klein shirt had a ketchup stain on it. Still, I put them on.

"Hey, Dave," he said at his door half an hour later. And patted me on the shoulder. Eric was drinking a Corona; had put *Sergeant Pepper's Lonely Hearts Club Band* on the stereo.

"Hey, Eric. You're certainly looking good." By which I meant he looked awake. He'd washed his hair, put on fresh clothes. On top of which he smelled soapy and young in that way that no cologne can replicate.

"I feel good," Eric said. "Last night I slept fourteen hours. Before that, I hadn't slept in a week." He motioned me upstairs. "And you? What have you been up to? Hard at work on another bestseller?"

"Oh, in a manner of speaking."

We went into his room, where he shuffled through the pile of papers on his desk. "Here it is," he said after a few seconds. "I thought you'd want to see this." And he handed me my paper.

On the back, in a very refined script, Mary Yearwood had written the following:

> Eric: I must confess that as I finish reading your paper, I find myself at something of a loss for words. It is really first-rate writing. Your analysis of both texts is graceful and subtle, in addition to which — and this is probably what impresses me most — you incorporate biographical and historical evidence into your argument in a manner that enriches the reader's understanding of the novels (in my view *Daisy Miller* must be looked upon as a novel) without ever seeming to intrude on their integrity as works of art. Also, your handling of the (homo)sexual underpinnings in both the James and Forster *oeuvres* is extremely deft, never polemical. And that extraordinary early poem of Forster's! Wherever did you find it? I applaud your research skills as well as your sensitivity to literary nuance.
>
> Looking back at your midterm, I have trouble believing the same student wrote this paper. Never in my career have I seen such a growth spurt. Clearly the tension of the exam room strangles your creativity (as it did mine). Therefore I have decided to exempt you from the final. The paper, thought out quietly in privacy, is the form for you, and so I shall assess your future performance purely on that basis.
>
> Last but not least, if you're not averse, I'd like to nomi-

nate this paper for several departmental prizes. And if you have a chance, why don't you stop by my office hours next week? Have you thought of graduate school? I'd like to discuss the possibility with you.

Grade: A

I put the paper down.

"So?" Eric said.

"I guess she liked it," I said.

"Liked it! She went apeshit." Kicking off his shoes, he sat down on the bed and started working on a joint. "You know, when I first read that part about the midterm, I choked. I thought, Shit, she'll say it's too good, someone else must have done it. But she didn't. She bought it!"

"I tried hard to make it sound, you know, like something a very smart college junior might write. I mean, as opposed to something Elizabeth Hardwick or Susan Sontag might write."

"And now I don't even have to take the final!" He laughed almost brutally. "*Stan-ford Biz School, here I come!* You really slung it, Dave."

"Well," I said.

My pulse quickened.

Very casually he put down the joint, unbuttoned and took off his shirt. Then his T-shirt.

He lay back. What a friend of mine called a "crab ladder" of hairs crawled from his belt up over his navel to disappear between small, brown nipples.

He lit the joint, took a puff.

"Dave Leavitt, come on down," he said. "You're the next contestant on the new *Price Is Right.*"

He started taking off his socks.

"Let me do that for you," I said.

And did. I licked his feet.

Above me, I heard him exhale. Reaching up, I felt his warm stomach rise and fall.

"Eric," I said.

"What?"

"I want to ask you something. I know it wasn't part of the bargain. Even so —"

"You can't fuck me," he said.

"No, not that. What I'd like to do — I'd like to kiss you."

"Kiss me!" He laughed. "Okay, sure. As your bonus for getting me out of the final."

I pulled myself up to shadow his face with my own; licked the acrid flavor of the pot from his tongue; sucked his soft, thick lips.

"You're a good kisser," I said after a few minutes.

"So they tell me."

"Who, girls?"

"Yeah."

"And how do I kiss, compared to girls?"

"Not bad, I guess."

"Afterwards, you'll have to tell me if I do something else better than girls do."

"To tell the truth, I'm kind of curious to find out myself," Eric said.

Then for about half an hour, though he made other noises, he didn't speak a word.

II.

THINGS STARTED LOOKING UP. My editor moved from Viking Penguin to Houghton Mifflin, which decided to bring out the paperback of *While England Sleeps,* as well as my new novel. "So it's a done deal," my agent said on the phone. "Oh, and by the way, I'm putting down a March of ninety-six delivery. Is that feasible?"

"Sure," I said. "Why not? I'm working harder than I have in years." Which was true. The quarter was drawing to a close, and I had two term papers to finish: "Mirror Imagery in Virginia Woolf" for Mary Yearwood, plus "Changing Attitudes toward Sex and Sexuality in 1890s England" for European History. Also, the day before I'd come home from the library only to get a message that someone named Hunter had called. Needless to say, I'm not of the generation that knows many people named Hunter. Still, I called back. Hunter told me he was a sophomore, a buddy of one of Eric's roommates. Could I meet him for lunch at the Fatburger on Santa Monica? he wanted to know. He had a business proposition to discuss.

Of course I went. Hunter turned out to be one of those muscular blond California boys who drive Jeeps and really do call every male person they know except maybe their fathers "dude."

"I'm a friend of Eric's," he began.

"Oh?"

He nodded. "And we were partying the other night, and I was telling him I was up shit creek with my World War II history paper, so he goes, 'Why don't you call up this dude I know, Dave Leavitt?'"

"He did."

"That's right. He said, well, that you could help me out. I mean, how am I supposed to finish this history paper, *and* my comp sci project, *and* my poli sci project, in addition to which I've got this huge econ final? Huge." Hunter took an enormous bite out of his Fatburger. "You understand my problem, dude?"

"Sure," I said. "As long as you understand my arrangement with Eric."

"I'm listening."

"I mean, did he explain to you how he, well, pays me?"

"Yeah."

"And are you willing to pay the same way?"

He crossed his arms. "Why not? I'm open-minded."

Mimicking his gesture, I sat back and looked him over. He didn't seem to mind. He had dark skin, longish blond hair brushed back over his ears, abundant blond chest hair, tufts of which poked upward from the collar of his shirt. An unintelligent handsomeness, unlike Eric's. Nor did he provoke in me anything like the ample sense of affection Eric had sparked from the first moment we'd met. Still, there is something to be said for the gutter lusts, and so far as these were concerned, Hunter possessed the necessary attributes — muscles, vulgarity, big hands — in abundance.

"So what's the assignment?" I asked.

"That's the trouble. I've got to find my own topic."

"History of the Second World War, right?" I thought. "Well, something that's always interested me is the story of the troops of black American soldiers who built Bailey bridges in Florence after the armistice."

"Bailey what?"

"Temporary bridges to replace the ones that were bombed."

"Cool. Professor Graham's black. He'll like that."

"Almost nothing's been written about those soldiers. Still, I could do some research —"

"It's supposed to be a research paper," Hunter added helpfully.

"When's it due?"

"That's the bitch. The twenty-first."

"The twenty-first!"

"I know, but what can I do? I only found out about you yesterday."

"I'm not sure I can manage a research paper by the twenty-first."

"Dude, please!"

He smiled, his mouth some orthodontist's pride.

I don't know what came over me, then: a lustful malevolence, you might call it, that made me want to see just how far I could go with this stupid, sexy, immoral boy.

"All right," I said. "There's just one condition. With this time constraint, the terms are going to have to be — how shall I put it? — more exacting than usual."

Hunter put his elbows on the table. "What did you have in mind?" he asked.

"Okay, how does this sound? Just to be fair, if you get a C or lower on the paper, you don't have to do anything. If you get a B, it's the same as with Eric: I give you a blow job. But if you get an A —"

"You can't fuck me," Hunter said.

Why did these boys all assume I wanted to fuck them?

"That wasn't what I was going to propose," I said. "What I was going to propose was . . . the opposite."

"That I fuck you?"

I nodded.

"Sure," Hunter said swiftly. "No problem."

"Have you ever fucked another guy?"

"No, but I have, you know, fucked a girl . . . back there."

"You have."

"Uh-huh."

"And did you like it?"

"Well . . ." He grinned. "I mean, it felt good and all, but afterwards — it *is* kind of gross to think about. You know what I'm saying?"

I coughed. "Well, I guess it's a done deal, Hunter."

"Great."

We shook.

"Oh, and Hunter," I added (what possessed me?), "just one more thing. There is the matter of a security deposit."

"Security deposit?"

"Didn't Eric tell you?"

"No."

"Well, naturally I require a security deposit. On my work. I'm sure you understand that."

"Sure, but what . . . kind of security deposit?"

I gestured for him to lean closer.

"Do you wear boxers or briefs?" I whispered.

"Depends. Today briefs."

"Good. All right, here's what I want you to do. I want you to go into the bathroom, into the toilet stall, and take off your pants and underwear. Then I want you to jack off into your underwear. You know, use them to wipe up. Then I want you to put them in your coat pocket. You can give them to me when we get outside."

"But —"

"You don't have to worry, there are locks on the stalls."

"But Eric didn't —"

"Or we could just forget the whole thing . . ."

He grimaced. Suddenly an expression of genuine disgust clouded his handsome face, so forcefully that for a moment I feared he might knock over the table, scream obscenities, hit or kill me.

Then the expression changed. He stood up.

"Back in a flash," he said, and strode into the bathroom.

Exactly five minutes later — I checked my watch — the bathroom door swung open.

"Ready?"

"Ready."

We headed out into the parking lot.

"Here you go, dude." Surreptitiously Hunter handed me a wad of white cotton.

My fingers brushed sliminess as I stuffed it into my pocket.

"And are you always that quick?"

"Only when I need to be."

He climbed into his Jeep and switched the radio on loud.

"So I'll have the paper for you the afternoon of the twentieth," I shouted over the noise.

"Sounds like a winner."

"Oh, and incidentally, Hunter, if you don't mind, maybe you could do it in the back of your Jeep."

"Do what?"

"If you get an A."

"Oh, man!" Hunter laughed. "Shit, you have really got a

filthy mind. I like it." Then he nearly slammed the door on my fingers.

Simple as that, I became an industry.

Days passed more quickly. I got up early in the mornings, sometimes as early as my father, who was usually weeding in the garden by six. Then I went to the library. Did you know that at the end of World War Two, after the Germans bombed the bridge of Santa Trinità in Florence, all four statues of the seasons which graced its corners were recovered from the river? Everything except spring's head. Posters went up, in which a photograph of the head appeared under the words, "Have You Seen This Woman? $3000.00 reward." Rumor had it that a black American soldier had kidnapped the head. Only no one ever turned up to claim the ransom.

Not until 1961 — the year I was born — was the head finally found, buried in mud at the bottom of the Arno.

Actually, I'd known this anecdote well before I started researching Hunter's paper. I'd even seen a reproduction of the poster itself when I'd gone to Florence a year earlier with Andy: heading into the Palazzo Medici-Riccardi one morning to look at Benozzo Gozzoli's frescoes of the *Procession of the Magi*, we'd stumbled on a photo exhibit commemorating the bombings that had nearly destroyed the city's medieval center. And there, amid the rubble-strewn piazzas and the women cheering the American liberators and the children in bread lines, the poster had hung, boldly American in its idioms, like the Wanted posters I used to study anxiously while my mother waited in line at the post office. Around it, in photographs, young black enlisted men — one of whom had been suspected of the theft — built Bailey bridges. If they felt the sting of injustice that must have been their daily lot in the military, their faces didn't show it. Instead, expressionless as ants, they heaved steel beams, and gradually restitched the severed city.

As I recall, Andy didn't take much notice of the soldiers. Good homosexual that he is, he was in a hurry to get over to the Accademia and see the David. And I should have been more interested in the David too; after all, he is my favorite sculpture, as well as the erotic ideal in pursuit of which Henry Somerset and his brethren had poured into Italy all those decades ago. And yet it was those soldiers — not the David — whose faces bloomed in my mind as we trudged up Via Ricasoli; to which I should add that I was in the middle of being sued then; in Italy, as it were, in flight from trouble; invention was almost painful to me. So why, at that particular moment, should a novel have started telling itself in my head? A novel I knew I could never write (and all the better)? A novel in which a young black soldier comes to Florence; from a distance, as he hammers planks, an Italian boy watches him, every morning, every afternoon . . .

The thing I need to emphasize is this: I never wanted to write that novel. I wanted just to muse on it as a possibility; listen to the story unfurling; drift with it, the way as a boy I used to keep up a running soap opera in my head. Every day I'd walk in circles around the pool outside our house in Stanford, bouncing a red rubber ball and spinning out in my mind elaborate and unending variations: pure plot. Sometimes I'd look up and see my mother watching me from the kitchen window. And when my ball got a hole in it, my father was always ready with his little packet of patches to seal it up.

A curious thing about my father: when, many years later, he moved down south, he gave away without compunction most of the sentimental objects of my childhood. Stuffed animals, Corgi cars, books. Yet he kept that ball. He still talks about it. "David's ball," he says, which I must have bounced a thousand miles in circles around that pool, in those days when invention was the simplest sort of pleasure or folly.

I think that was what I was trying to recapture: all the gratitude of authorship, with none of the responsibility implicit in signing one's name.

And how hard I worked! Mornings in the library, afternoons at my father's computer. For Eric's history project, I was able to cannibalize a good deal of the research I'd already done for the Somerset novel — that novel which, like the Bailey bridge novel, I was now certain I would never write. An essay I'd done in college on *Between the Acts* formed the basis for "Mirror Imagery in Virginia Woolf." And Hunter: well, thanks to that unwritten, even unwhispered bit of story, he ended up getting the best paper of all three.

And why was that? This is the thing of which, I suspect, I'm going to have the hardest time convincing you. After all, a bond of genuine affection united Eric and me: it made sense that I should want to do well by him. Toward Hunter, my feelings could best be described as an admixture of contempt and lust. Nor did he like me any better than I liked him. Contempt and lust: how is it possible that from such a devalued marriage as this, art could have been conceived? Yet it was. Indeed, as I look back, I recognize that there was something startlingly clear, even serene, about my partnership with Hunter, which no yearnings for domesticity defiled. Eric, on the other hand, I was always calling up and asking if he wanted to have lunch. He'd meet me when he had time, which was rarely, since lately he'd gotten busy with his juggling lessons.

Yes, juggling lessons.

Sometimes I'd go over to his house and lie on his bed,

stoned, while above his head he hurled three red pins, or three sticks, or three white balls. Only the occasional "shit" or "fuck" interrupted his quiet, huffing focus. A ball bounced toward the window, or the pins clattered. Then he picked up the pins and started fresh, as the dense odor of his sweat claimed the room.

He said he was hoping to get good enough to juggle on weekends for extra cash. He said he was working up to fire.

And need I mention that those evenings never evolved into the erotic? Of course one hoped. Yet Eric was scrupulous, and — more to the point — not that interested. Sex with me, to his view, was a reward for a job well done.

With Hunter, by contrast, sex was payment for services rendered. I hope I've made the distinction clearly.

And of course he got his A. I learned only from Eric, who'd gotten A's too and called me up before Christmas break to whoop about it. "Hasn't Hunter told you?" he asked when I inquired, and when I said no, went silent. Then I tried to phone Hunter, but he was never at home. This didn't surprise me, betrayal being the usual result when one starts making gentleman's agreements with people who are not gentlemen.

Anyway, what more should I have expected from a boy who buys a term paper, then tries to pass it off as his own?

In the end I had to track him down at the UCLA pool. Dripping chlorine, the golden hair on his chest made my mouth water. I wanted to drink him.

"Hey, I've been meaning to call you," he said as he toweled himself.

"I've been trying to call you too. You're never home."

"Sorry about that, dude. I've been busy. By the way, my professor really loved that paper! I appreciate it."

"No problem."

He dried under his arms.

"So anyway, the reason I'm here, Hunter, is that I'd like to know when you intend to fulfill your half of the bargain."

"Softer, your voice carries!"

"What, you don't want any of your friends to know I wrote your paper for you?"

"Softer!" He pushed me into a corner. "Look," he said, his whisper agitated, "it'll have to be after I'm back from break. Right now I'm too busy."

"No, it'll have to be before you leave for break. Didn't your mother teach you it's never a good idea to put things off?" I patted him on the arm. "Tell you what, why don't you come over to my dad's place tomorrow around noon? He's away for the weekend. We can put the Jeep in the garage."

"The Jeep!"

"You did get an A, Hunter."

"But I —"

"What, you thought I was just going to write that paper for nothing? Uh-uh. You be there at noon."

I gave him my address, after which he limped off toward the showers.

He was not a bad kid, really. It was just part of his affably corrupt nature to try to get away with things. Of such stuff as this are captains of industry made.

Probably the aspect of this story that puzzles me most, as I look back, is how word of my "availability" circulated so quickly through the halls and dormitories of UCLA those next months. I don't mean that it became common knowledge among the student body that David Leavitt, novelist, was available to write term papers for good-looking male undergraduates; no articles appeared in *The Daily Bruin,* or graffiti (so far as I am aware) on bathroom walls. Still, in a controlled way, news got out, and as the spring quarter opened, no less than five boys called me up with papers to be written. And how had they gotten my number in the first place? I tried to imagine the conversations that had taken place: "Shit, Eric, I don't know how I'm supposed to finish this paper on 'Ode to a Grecian Urn' by Friday." "Why don't you call up Dave Leavitt? He'll do it for you if you let him give you a blow job." "A blow job, huh? Sounds great. What's his number?"

Or perhaps the suggestion was never so direct. Perhaps it was made in a more discreet language, or a more vulgar one. The latter, I suspect. In fact I'm sure that at some point all the boys, even Eric, made rude, humiliating remarks about me, called me "faggot" or "cocksucker," then qualified those (to them) insults by adding that I was "still a basically decent guy." Or some such proviso.

Business got so good, I started turning down offers, either because I was overworked, or because the boy in question, when I met him, simply didn't appeal to me physically, in which case I would apologize and say that I couldn't spare the time. (I hated this part of the job, but what could I do? Profit was my motive, not charity. I never gave anything for which I didn't get something back.

You'd think I *had* gone to business school.)

All told, I wrote papers for seven boys — seven boys toward most of whom I felt something partway between the affection that ennobled my friendship with Eric and the contempt that characterized my dealings with Hunter. The topics ranged from "The Image of the Wanderer in English Romantic Poetry" to "The Fall of the Paris Commune" to "Child Abandonment in Medieval Italy" to "Flight in Toni Morrison's *Song of Solomon*" to "Bronzino and the Traditions of Italian Renaissance Portraiture."

Of these boys, and papers, the only other one I need to tell you about is Ben.

Ben got in touch with me around midterm of the spring quarter. "Mr. Leavitt?" he said on the phone. "My name's Ben Hollingsworth. I got your number from Tony Younger."

"Oh?"

"Yes. He told me to call you. He said you might . . . that we could —"

"Relax. There's no need to be nervous."

"Thanks. I'm really . . . I don't know where to start."

"Why don't we meet?" I offered, my voice as honeyed and professional as any prostitute's. "It's always easier to talk in person."

"Where?"

I suggested the Ivy, only Ben didn't want to meet at the Ivy — or any other public place, for that matter. Instead he asked if he could pick me up on the third floor of the Beverly Center parking lot, near the elevators. Then we could discuss things in his car.

I said that was fine by me.

We rendezvoused at ten-thirty the next morning. It was unusually chilly out. Ben drove a metallic blue Honda, the passenger door to which was dented. "Mr. Leavitt?" he asked as he threw it open.

"In the flesh."

I climbed in. Altogether, with his carefully combed black hair and short-sleeve button-down shirt (pen in breast pocket), he reminded me of those Mormon missionary boys you sometimes run into in the European capitals, with badges on their lapels that say "Elder Anderson" or "Elder Carpenter." And as it turned out, the association was prophetic. Ben *was* a Mormon, as I soon learned, albeit from Fremont, California, not Utah. No doubt in earlier years he'd done the very same European "service," handing out pamphlets to confused homosexual tourists who'd thought he might be cruising them.

"I really appreciate your taking the time to see me, Mr. Leavitt," he began as I put on my seat belt.

"Call me David."

"I'd feel more comfortable calling you Mr. Leavitt."

"Okay, whatever. And what should I call you?"

"Ben."

"Ben. Fine. Anyway, it's no problem."

We headed out of the parking lot. "I just want to make one thing clear," he said. "I want you to know that I've never cheated on anything in my life. Not a test, not a paper. And I've never stolen anything either. I don't drink, I've never used drugs. I'm a clean liver, Mr. Leavitt. I've had the same girlfriend since I was fifteen. And now here I am driving with you, and we're about to enter into an unholy alliance — at least I hope we are, because if we don't, my GPA will go below 3.5 and I need higher than that to get into a good law school. I'm so desperate that I'm willing to do things I'll be ashamed of for the rest of my life. You, I don't know if you're ashamed. It's none of my business."

We turned left onto San Vicente. "Probably not," I said.

"No. And it must sound terrible to you, what I'm suggesting. Still, the way I see it, there's no alternative because one day I'm going to have a family to support, and I've got to be ready. Most of these other guys, they've got rich parents to fall back on. I don't. And since I'm also not black or in a wheelchair or anything, it's that much more difficult. Do you hear what I'm saying? I don't really have any choice in the matter."

"You always have a choice, Ben."

Opening the window, he puffed out a visible sigh. Something in his square, scrubbed, slightly acned face, I must admit, excited me. His cock, I imagined, would taste like Dial soap. And yet even as Ben's aura of clean living excited me, his shame shamed me. After all, none of the other boys for whom I'd written papers had ever expressed the slightest scruple about passing off my work as their own; if anything, it was the sex part, the prostitutional part, that made them flinch. Which, when you came to think about it, was astounding: as if the brutal exigencies of the marketplace had ingested whole, in each of them, all shopworn, kindergarten notions of right and wrong.

In Ben, on the other hand, those same kindergarten notions seemed to exert just enough pressure to make him worry, though not quite enough to make him change his mind.

"So what's the class?" I asked.

"Victorian History."

"And the assignment?"

"Are you saying you'll do it?"

"You'll have to tell me what the assignment is first."

"Jack the Ripper," Ben said.

"Really? How funny. I was just reading about him."

"You were?"

"Yes. Apparently a lot of people thought he was Prince Eddy, Queen Victoria's grandson and the heir to the throne. Since then that's pretty much been disproven, though."

"Wow," Ben said. "That might be an interesting angle to

take . . . if you're interested. Are you interested? I hope you are, because if you're not I'll have to figure out something else, and buying a term paper with cash is something I just can't afford right now."

"Ben, slow down for a second. I have to say, this whole situation worries me. Are you sure you know what you're getting yourself into?"

"Do you mean do I understand what I'll have to do in exchange? Of course! Tony told me, I'll have to let you — you know — perform oral sex on me. And no, I can't pretend I'm comfortable with it. But I'm willing. Like I said, I have this girlfriend, Jessica. I've never cheated on her, either."

We stopped at a red light, where Ben opened his wallet. From between fragile sheets of plastic, a freckled girl with red hair smiled out at us.

"Very pretty," I said.

"She will be the mother of my children," Ben said reverently.

Then he put the picture away, as if continued exposure to my gaze might blight it.

The light changed.

"Of course, if you say no because I'm not so good-looking as Tony, well, there's nothing I can do about that. Still, I do have rather a large penis. I understand homosexuals like large penises. Is that true?"

"Sometimes." Laughing, I patted his knee. "Look, you know what I think? I think *you* should write your paper. And I'll read it over for you, how does that sound? Free of charge, as it were. And if you do get a C in history, well, so what? It won't matter in the long run. And meanwhile you won't have cheated on Jessica, or compromised your ethics."

"But I'm fully prepared to compromise my ethics." Ben's voice grew panicked. "Also the security deposit. Tony told me about that too, and I've already taken care of it. Look."

Reaching across my lap, he opened the glove compartment. A bleachy odor of semen wafted from the opening.

Pulling out a pair of rumpled boxer shorts, Ben tossed them into my lap.

"When did you do this?" I asked, caressing slick cotton.

"Just now. Just before I picked you up." He grinned. "So what do you say, Mr. Leavitt? Will you do it?"

"All right." My mouth was dry.

"That's great. That's terrific."

He turned onto Saturn Street.

I wiped my fingertips on my jeans.

As I'd told Ben, I already knew a little about Jack the Ripper. This was because Prince Eddy, whose candidature for the post "Ripperologists" were forever bandying about, stood also at the center of the Cleveland Street scandal. Indeed, several historians believed that Lord Arthur Somerset had fled England primarily to take the heat off Eddy (also a regular client at the brothel) as a favor to his old friend and protector the prince of Wales.

It would have been interesting, I thought, to write a paper linking Prince Eddy's homosexuality with the hatred of the female body that seemed to have been such a motivating element in the Ripper crimes. Unfortunately, fairly hard proof existed that Eddy had been off shooting in Scotland on the date of two of the murders, and since Ben's assignment was to make a strong case for one suspect or another, I decided I'd better look elsewhere. M. J. Druitt, a doctor whose body was found floating in the Thames about seven weeks after the last murder, was certainly the candidate toward whom most of the evidence pointed. Yet for this reason, it seemed likely that many of Ben's classmates would argue for Druitt.

Who else then? Among the names that came up most frequently were those of Frank Miles, with whom Oscar Wilde had once shared a house; Virginia Woolf's cousin James Stephen, who had been Eddy's tutor; the painter Walter Sickert; and Queen Victoria's private physician, Sir William Gull. Indeed, a large percentage of the suspects seemed to have been physicians, which is no surprise: to disembowel a woman's body as precisely as the Ripper did that of Mary Kelly, you would have to possess a detailed knowledge of human anatomy. And if Donald Rumbelow is correct in proposing that the Ripper's weapon was a postmortem knife "with a thumb-grip on the blade which is specifically designed for 'ripping' upwards," the evidence that he was a medical man appears even stronger.

So: the Ripper as doctor, or anti-doctor. As far as this "angle" went, the argument that intrigued me the most came from someone called Leonard Matters, who in 1929 had published a book claiming that the Ripper was in fact a "Dr. Stanley." His brilliant young son having died of a venereal infection after traveling to Paris with a prostitute named Mary Kelly, this good doctor (according to Matters's theory) had gone mad and started scouring the alleys of Whitechapel, bent on revenging himself not only against Mary Kelly, but prostitutes in general.

A second possibility was to talk about class. This struck me as an interesting if somewhat experimental approach because regardless of who actually committed the crimes, the Victorian imagination — of which gossip is the strongest echo — associated Jack almost obsessively with Buckingham Palace. If he was not a member of the royal family, then he was someone close to the royal family, some mad failure of stately blood who would periodically troll the streets of East London in search of whores to murder and eviscerate. And couldn't that be looked upon as an allegory for the exploitation of the working classes by the upper classes through history? A Marxist argument proposed itself. After all, as victims Jack chose exclusively prostitutes of an extremely degraded type: older women, alcoholic, with too many children and no qualms about lifting their petticoats in a squalid alley to pay for a drink. To write about the Ripper as a personification of the bourgeoisie's contempt for the workers would certainly provide a provocative twist on the assignment. Or perhaps such a twist would be *too* provocative, especially coming from a boy like Ben.

A third possibility was to talk about xenophobia: for if the Ripper suspects could be categorized, then the last rough category (after doctors and aristocrats) was immigrants.

And as I mulled over each of these angles, the one thing I could not get out of my mind was a police photograph I'd seen of the corpse of Mary Kelly, the last of Jack's victims and the only one to be killed in her room. Her body had been found on the bed, quite literally split down the middle. The nose had been cut off, the liver sliced out and placed between the feet. The kidneys, breasts, and the flesh from the thighs had been dumped on the bedside table, and the hand inserted into the stomach.

Even in my own epoch of serial killers and snuff films, of Charles Manson and Jeffrey Dahmer, I'd never seen anything quite like that.

Three days passed in research. Each morning I'd wake vowing to conclude the afternoon with a decision, and each afternoon I'd go home having failed. Then only a week remained before Ben's paper was due, and I hadn't even started writing. It felt as if something had seized up in me, the way the screen of a computer will sometimes freeze into immobility. Nor did it help when Ben stopped by my carrel one afternoon to give me a book I'd already read and returned. "It's called *The Identity of Jack the Ripper,*" he said. "And according to this guy, at first they thought the Ripper was a Polish barber who went by the name of George Chapman, but then they found out that he had a double, a *Russian* barber, and that this double —"

"Also sometimes used the name Chapman. I know."

"Oh, you've already read it? Well, never mind, then. I just thought in case you hadn't —"

"Thanks."

"Say, you want a Seven-Up or something?"

I said why not.

We repaired to the vending machines, then taking our drinks outside, sat on a bench in the library courtyard. It was a warm spring day, better than most only in that the air was unusually clear. A breeze even seemed to carry the scent of mountains.

For a time the only noise in that courtyard, aside from the buzz of yellow jackets, was the pop of our drink cans opening. Then Ben said, "Strange, all this."

"What?"

"Just . . . our sitting together."

"Why?"

"I'm not sure quite how to explain. You see, in the church — did I tell you I'm a Mormon?"

"No."

"Well, in the church we have this very clear-cut conception of sin. And so I always assumed that if I ever committed a really big sin, like we're doing now . . . I don't know, that there'd be a clap of thunder and God would strike me dead or something. Instead of which we're sitting here in this courtyard and the sun's shining. The grass is green."

"But what's the sin?"

"You know. Cheating."

"Is cheating really a sin?"

"Of course. It's part of lying."

"Well," I said, "then maybe the fact that the sun's shining and the grass is green means God doesn't really care that much. Or maybe God doesn't exist."

Ben's face convulsed in horror.

"Just a possibility," I added.

Ben leaned back in disillusion. "So you're an atheist," he said. "I suppose I should have expected it. I suppose I should have guessed most homosexuals would be atheists."

"Oh, some homosexuals are very religious. In fact, it wouldn't surprise me to find out one or two were actually Mormons."

"Ex-Mormons."

"A lot more than two of those. But to get back to what you were saying, I wouldn't call myself an atheist. Instead I'd say I'm a skeptical lapsed Jew, distrustful of dogma."

"Tony's Jewish too. Last night he was telling me about his circumcision —"

"His *bris.*"

"— and how in Israel they use the foreskins to make fertility drugs." He shook his head in wonder.

"Are you circumcised, Ben?"

"No, actually." Blushing, he checked his watch.

We got up and walked toward the library. "Well, back to the salt mines," Ben said at the main doors. "By the way, I hope you realize I'm working my butt off too. I really bit off more than I could chew this quarter."

"Oh, I'll bet you can chew more than you think."

"Probably. Still, I wanted to make sure you knew. I mean, I wouldn't want you thinking that the whole time you were sweating out this paper, I was playing pinball or something." He wiped his nose. "By the way, have you decided who did it yet?"

"Not yet. The problem is, everyone has a different theory about the Ripper, and every theory has a hole in it." Which was true. Indeed, looked at collectively, the theories ramified so far afield that the actual murders began to seem beside the point. For if you believed them all, then the Ripper was Prince Eddy *and* Walter Sickert. The Ripper was Frank Miles *and* M. J. Druitt *and* Sir William Gull. The Ripper was an *agent provocateur* sent by the Russian secret police to undermine the reputation of their London brethren. The Ripper was a Jewish *shochet,* or ritual slaughterer, suffering from a religious mania. The Ripper was a high-level conspiracy to squelch a secret marriage between Prince Eddy and a poor Catholic girl. The Ripper was Jill the Ripper, an abortionist betrayed by a guilt-ridden client and sent to prison, and therefore bent on avenging herself on her own sex.

Not to mention the black magician and the clique of Freemasons and (how could I forget him?) Virginia Woolf's cousin (and possibly Prince Eddy's lover), the handsome, demented James Stephen.

But which one? Or all of them?

Saying goodbye to Ben, I returned to my carrel. As it happened I'd left the photograph of Mary Kelly's corpse lying open on the desk. And how curious! As I sat down, that "butcher's shambles" no longer made me nauseated. Perhaps one really can get used to anything.

And upon this degraded body of the late nineteenth century, I thought, *some real demon swooped, ransacking its cavities like a thief in search of hidden jewels, and finding instead only a panic, an emptiness, a vacancy.*

But what demon? Who?

I looked up.

Modernism and espionage, Diaspora and homosexuality, religious mania and anti-Semitism and most vividly — to me most vividly — desire and disease, gruesomely coupled.

"Fantastic," I said. For all at once — sometimes inspiration really is all at once — I saw who Ben's Ripper had to be.

The Ripper was the spirit of the twentieth century itself.

I worked fast those next days, faster than I'd ever worked on anything else. Looking back, I see that the pleasure I experienced as I wrote that paper lay in its contemplation as a completed object, like the Bailey bridge novel I was sure I would never begin. Or a Bailey bridge, for that matter. Bank to bank I built, and as I did a destination, a connection, neared. It was the same end I'd hoped to reach in my Somerset book: a sort of poeticization of that moment when the soul of my own century, the soul of vacancy itself, devoured the last faithful remnants of an age that had believed, almost without question, in presences.

After that, from the unholy loins of Jack the Ripper, whole traditions of alienation had been spilled, of which I was merely one exemplary homunculus. Eric was another: Eric with his cheerful, well-intentioned immorality. And Hunter. Even Ben. We were the nightmare Mary Kelly had dreamed the night she was murdered.

I finished, to my own surprise, three days early. That same afternoon my agent called. "Congratulate me," I said. "I've just done the best work of my life."

"Congratulations," Andrew said. "Now when do I get to see pages?" To which request I responded, rather unconvincingly, "Soon."

How could I have explained to him that the only thing that made it possible for me to write those pages was the knowledge that they would never bear my name?

I called Ben. He sounded happy and surprised at my news, and as before we arranged to meet on the third floor of the Beverly Center parking lot.

He was waiting in his car when I pulled up. "Nice to see you, Mr. Leavitt," he said.

"Nice to see you too, Ben." I climbed in. "Beautiful day, isn't it?"

"Mm." He was staring expectantly at my briefcase.

"Oh, the paper," I said, taking it out and handing it to him.

"Great," Ben said. "Let's go up to the roof and I'll read it."

"Read it?"

"What, you think I'm going to turn in a paper I haven't read?" He shook his head in wonderment, then inserting the key in the ignition, drove us up into sunlight. To be honest, I was a little surprised: after all, none of the other boys for whom I'd written had ever felt the need to verify the quality of my work. (Then again none of the other boys had been remotely scrupulous in the second sense of the word, either.) Still, I couldn't deny Ben the right to look over something that was going to be turned in under his name; in addition to which the prospect of seeing his astounded face as he reached the end of my last paragraph did rather thrill me; even in such a situation as this, I still had my writer's vanity. So I sat there, my ripper's eyes fixed on the contoured immensity in his polyester slacks, and only balked when he took a pen from his shirt pocket and crossed out a line.

"What are you doing?"

"I just think this sentence about Druitt is a bit redundant. Look."

I looked. It was redundant.

"But you can't turn in a paper all marked up like that!"

"What, you thought I was going to turn in this copy? Are you kidding? No way! I'll type it over tonight on my own computer."

He returned to his reading. Periodically he jotted a note in the margin, or drew a line through a word or phrase. All of which made me so nervous, he might have been Michiko Kakutani sitting in the next seat, reviewing one of my novels while I watched.

Finally Ben put the paper down.

"Well?" I said.

"Well . . ." He scratched his head with his pen. "It's very interesting, Mr. Leavitt. Very . . . imaginative. The only thing is, I'm not sure it answers the assignment."

"How so?"

"The assignment was to make a case for someone or other being Jack the Ripper. And basically, what you're saying is that it doesn't matter. That any of them, or all of them, could have been Jack the Ripper."

"Exactly."

"But that's not what Professor Robinson asked for."

I spread my hands patiently on my lap. "I understand what's worrying you, Ben. Still, try to think about it this way. You have a murder mystery, right? A whodunit. Only there's no clear evidence that any one person did it. So the B student thinks, I'll just make a case for the most likely suspect and be done with it. But the A student thinks, More is going on here than meets the eye. The A student thinks, I've got to use this as an opportunity to investigate a larger issue."

"I can see all that. Still, this stuff about twentieth-century modernism — I have to be honest with you, Mr. Leavitt, to me it sounds a little pretentious."

"Pretentious!"

"I mean, very intelligent and all. Only the spirit of twentieth-century modernism — that can't hold a knife. That can't strangle someone. And so I'm afraid Professor Robinson will think it's — I don't know — off-the-wall."

Clearly Ben had the limited vision of the B student.

"Well, I'm sorry you're disappointed," I said.

"Oh, I'm not disappointed exactly! It just wasn't what I expected."

"Fine. Then I'll go home this afternoon and rewrite it. You just have to tell me who you think actually did do it —"

"Mr. Leavitt —"

"Was it M. J. Druitt, or James Stephen, or Dr. Pedechenko? Or how about Jill? It could have been Jill."

Ben was silent.

Then: "Mr. Leavitt, you can't blame me for being worried. A lot rests on this paper for me. You, you've got nothing to lose."

Was that true?

"And *you* don't risk expulsion if you get caught."

"Well, naturally, and that's exactly why I'm offering to rewrite it." (My anger had dissipated.) "After all, Ben, you're the customer, and the customer's —"

"Do you have to make it sound so . . . commercial?"

"Isn't it?"

"I'm not sure," Ben said. "I never have been."

Once again he took out his pen. From the bottom of his breast pocket, I noticed, a tear-shaped blue ink stain seeped downward. "You must have put your pen away without the cap," I said.

"Did I? I guess. I do it all the time."

"Me too."

With my forefinger, I stroked the stain. Ben's breathing quickened.

"Look," he said, "about the paper. You don't have to rewrite it. I mean, if I didn't appreciate it, it probably says more about me than about you, right?"

"Not necessarily —"

"And anyway, I didn't come to you to get a B paper, I came to you to get an A paper. And if I don't recognize an A paper when I see one, all that points up are my limitations."

"Maybe." I moved my finger downward, to brush the cleft of his chest. "Or maybe it only points up the fact that I have a wider experience of these things. Remember, I've never gotten anything less than an A on a paper in my life — for myself or anyone else."

"Mr. Leavitt, please don't touch me like that. Someone might see us."

"I'm sorry." I took my hand away.

"Thank you," Ben said, clearing his throat. "And now I guess I owe you something, don't I?"

"Oh, don't worry about that. For that let's just wait until you get your grade. Then we can —"

"No, I'd rather get it over with, if you don't mind. Not have it hanging over my head." He played with his collar. "Obviously we can't do it here. Where can we do it?"

"My dad's place," I said swiftly. "He and his wife are in Singapore."

Without a word, Ben switched on the ignition and drove me back to my car. "Follow me," I said, and he did, down Santa Monica to Cahuenga and Barham, then onto the 134, the flat, trafficked maze of the Inland Empire.

Around one-thirty we pulled into my father's garage. "Come on in," I said, switching off the burglar alarm. "Make yourself at home. You want to take a swim in the pool first?"

"I didn't bring a suit."

"You don't need one. No one will see you but me."

"Actually," Ben said, "I'd rather just — you know — get down to business, if that's all right with you."

"Fine," I said. "It's this way." And we headed together down the long corridor into my bedroom.

"This is nice."

"Thanks. It's not really mine. Just the guest room. But I try to put in some personal touches when I'm here. That little painting, for instance. My friend Arnold Mesches did it."

"What is it, a turkey?"

"A portrait of a turkey."

"That's funny."

I took off my shoes. "By the way, would you rather I leave the lights on or off?"

"Off."

"All cats are gray in the dark, right? All right, then, why don't you just . . . take your clothes off and lie down on the bed. And I'll be back in a minute."

"Okay."

Like a discreet masseur, I stepped into the bathroom, where I brushed my teeth and got out some condoms. Then I walked back in. Ben was sitting naked on the edge of the bed, shivering a little.

"Are you cold?" I asked.

He shook his head.

"Wow," I said, sitting down next to him. "Lucky I've got extra-large condoms."

He wrapped his arms around his chest. "Mr. Leavitt, you embarrass me when you say things like that."

"Look, Ben," I said, trying to sound paternal, "I've been thinking about it, and if you don't want to —"

"No, it's okay."

"But it's also okay if you don't want to. I mean, you can still have the paper. Don't tell Tony, though." I winked.

"What's his like?" Ben's voice was surprisingly urgent.

"Tony's? Oh. Fine. Smaller than yours, of course."

"Straight or curved?"

"Straight."

"The other night he was telling me that in his fraternity, they take the pledges and shave their balls."

"Yeah?"

"If they pass out from too much drinking."

Something occurred to me. "You're not in a fraternity, are you, Ben?"

"No."

I brushed my fingers against his scrotum.

"Your balls are pretty hairy. I could shave them for you, if you wanted." I hesitated. "You know, we could pretend you were the pledge."

Ben started shaking.

"Or that I was Tony —"

"Shut up."

And pulling my face toward his, he thrust his tongue down my throat.

Don't think he wanted me. He didn't. Yes, he stayed that night, allowed me to initiate him into even the most specialized modes of intimacy — and initiated me into one or two as well. Yet as we sat down across from each other at breakfast the next morning, I could tell from his eyes that it wasn't me he was thinking about. Maybe Jessica, or God. Probably Tony. Not me.

He left shortly thereafter, having first extracted from me a promise never to tell anyone what had happened between us — a promise I naturally kept. And as I watched his car disappear onto California Boulevard, I couldn't guess whether he'd ever do it again, or do it only once again, or change his life and do it a thousand times. I knew only that during our night together, the marrow of identity had been touched. Whether it had been altered, however, I couldn't say.

A lull ensued. Spring break took most UCLA boys to a beach. With my father and Jean still in the Orient, I resorted to old habits: an hour each morning at the library, followed by Book Soup and lunch at the Mandarette Café. Then Andy was back in town for a few days between shoots; and my friend Matt Wolf from London. I got busy.

Something like my old life claimed me.

Naturally I was curious to find out, when spring break ended, what grade Ben had gotten on his paper; also, whether he'd bother to call and tell me what grade he'd gotten on his paper.

When finally I heard news of the matter, however (this was early April), it wasn't from Ben but from Eric.

Eric and I hadn't been in touch much lately. My suspicion was that he had a new girlfriend, the sort of thing he would never have discussed with me. So I was surprised and happy when he called me up one Sunday morning at seven and ordered me to meet him for breakfast at Ships on La Cienega.

He was waiting in a corner booth when I got there. A placid, sleepy smile on his face, he held the menu with fingers marked by little burns. "Juggling fire?" I asked.

"I got fifty bucks on Venice Beach last Sunday," Eric said.

"Congratulations." And I sat down. His skin was porphyry-colored from the sun.

"I must say, I never expected to hear from you at seven in the morning," I said. "You're not usually such an early riser."

"Depends on the season. Anyway, I had some news to tell you."

"Tell me."

"I just thought you should know, apparently some guy you wrote for — Ben something — got caught last week."

"Caught?"

"Tony Younger called me. Banana waffles for two," he added to the waitress, "and another cup of coffee. Anyway, yes. Apparently what happened was that when this guy Ben got back from spring break he found a message waiting from his history professor, the gist of which was to get over to her office hours pronto. So he went, and she basically told him that after reading his paper, and comparing it with his other papers, she'd come to the conclusion that it wasn't his own work. Too sophisticated or something. Then she gave him a choice. Either he could admit he hadn't written the paper, in which case he'd get a C and the incident would be dropped, or he could protest, in which case he'd get an F and the whole thing brought before the honor board."

"Damn. What did he choose?"

"That's the clincher. Apparently this Ben, this idiot, not only confessed he hadn't written the paper, he practically got down on his knees and started begging the professor's forgiveness. Tony's roommate was outside the office, he heard the whole thing." Eric shook his head in disgust. "After that he went straight to his room, packed up his things, and left. And since then — this was three days ago — no one, not even Tony, who's one of his best friends, has heard a word from him."

"Eric," I said, "I have to ask. Did he mention me?"

"Always thinking about others, aren't you, Dave? But no, he didn't."

"As if it matters. As if it makes it any less my fault."

"Hey, take it easy." The waffles arrived. "You're too quick to blame yourself," Eric went on, pouring syrup. "I mean, it's not as if this Ben guy didn't know the risks. He came to *you.* Don't forget that. And he could have fought it. Me, I would have said" — his voice went high — "'Miss Yearwood, Miss Yearwood, how can you think I'd *do* something like that!' And cried or something. Whereas he just gave in. You can't break down like that! The way I see it, they're testing you twenty-four hours a day. They want to see if you can sweat it out. If Ben couldn't take the pressure, it's not your problem. Still, I'd say it's probably better if you kept a low profile around campus for a while." He patted my hand. "Me, I'm lucky. I've finished my humanities requirements. And if I win a prize for that paper, it'll go a long way toward Stanford Biz School, provided I get a high enough score on my GMATs. Did I tell you I have GMATs coming up?"

He hadn't — a lapse he now corrected in lavish detail — after which we said goodbye in the parking lot, Eric cheerful as he drove off into his happy future, me wretched as I contemplated the ruin of Ben's academic career, a ruin for which, no matter what Eric might say to assuage my guilt, I understood myself to be at least in part responsible. For suddenly it didn't matter that I hadn't gotten caught; it didn't matter that no one knew what I had done except the boys themselves, none of whom would ever squeal on me. Because I had written my paper, and not Ben's, he had suffered. Blame could not be averted. The best I could do was try to bear it with valor.

I got into my father's car. For some reason I was remembering a moment years before, in elementary school, when a girl called Michele Fox had put before me an ethical dilemma familiar to most American schoolchildren at that time: if a museum were burning down, she'd said, and you could save either the old lady or the priceless art treasure, which would you choose? Well, I'd answered, it depends. Who is the old lady? What is the art treasure? To which she responded — wisely, I'm sure — "You're missing the point, David Leavitt." No doubt I was missing the point — her point — since Michele had few doubts in life. (She grew up to be a 911 operator.) As for me, I tortured that little conundrum for years, substituting for the generic old lady first my aunt Ida, then Eudora Welty; for the priceless treasure first the Mona Lisa, then Picasso's *Guernica.* Each time my answer was different. Sometimes I opted for life, sometimes for art. And how surprising! From this capriciousness a philosophy formed itself in me, according to which only particularities — not generalities — counted. For principles are rarely human things, and when museums burn — when any buildings burn — the truth is, most people save themselves.

What I'm trying to say here is, I made no effort to get in touch with, or help, Ben. Instead, that afternoon, I booked a flight to New York, where by the end of the week I was once again installed in that real life from which the episode of the term papers now turns out to have been merely a long and peculiar divagation.

III.

I RAN INTO BEN ABOUT A YEAR LATER. This was in the Uffizi Gallery, in Florence, where I'd gone to research (I am actually now writing it) my Bailey bridge novel. I was looking at Bronzino's portrait of Eleonora di Toledo, and Ben was looking at Bronzino's portrait of the baby Giovanni, fat-cheeked and clutching his little sparrow, and then, quite suddenly, we were looking at each other.

"Ben?" I said, not sure at first that it was he.

"Mr. Leavitt!" To my relief, he smiled.

We walked upstairs, where in the little coffee bar on the roof, I bought him a cappuccino. Ben looked better than he had when we'd first known each other. For one thing, his hair was both longer and messier, which suited him; also, he'd foregone his old Mormon uniform in favor of denim, down, hiking boots: ordinary clothes, boy clothes, in which his body, somehow ampler-seeming, rested with visible ease. Nor did he appear in the least surprised to be sitting with me there. "Actually," he said, "since I've been in Florence I've bumped into six people I knew from school. It might as well be Westwood Village." He took a sip from his cappuccino. "I never knew coffee could be so good before I came to Italy."

"How long have you been here?"

"In Florence, three days. In Italy, two weeks. I'm with my friend. No — I guess I should say my lover." He leaned closer. "Keith and I talk about this all the time. Lover's stupid, and friend's too euphemistic, and partner sounds like a business arrangement. So Keith says, 'Just say you're with Keith.' But then people say, 'Who's Keith?' And I'm back to square one."

"Well, you don't have to worry with me," I said, smiling. "Anyway, how did you meet Keith?"

"It was after I quit school, while I was living with my parents in Fremont. The thing was, I just kept having this yen to go into San Francisco. The usual story. So one night I was driving up and down Castro Street, and finally I worked up the courage to stop in at a bar. The next thing I knew someone was buying me a beer."

"And that was Keith?"

"Oh no. Keith came later." Ben's cheeks reddened. "He likes to tell people we met at a party, but the truth is we met on the street. He cruised me, we went back to his apartment and fucked. The rest is history." Ben drained his coffee cup. "And what about you, Mr. Leavitt? What have you been up to this year? Still living with your father?"

"No, I'm back in New York."

"Oh, great. And who are you writing term papers for there? NYU boys? Columbia boys?"

"Actually, I'm working on a novel."

"Better, I guess." His tone was somehow reproachful and affectionate all at once.

We were quiet for a moment. Then I said, "Ben, about that paper —"

"So you heard what happened."

"Yes. And I'm sorry. Probably you were right, probably it was pretentious. Or at least, not the right thing for you. I always tried to make my papers sound like they came from the people they were supposed to be coming from. I guess in your case, though, I got carried away. Infatuated, almost. The thing was, I fell in love with an idea."

"You're a writer. Writers are supposed to fall in love with ideas."

"Exactly. And that's why I should have been more careful. After all, if I'd done the paper the way you'd asked me to —"

"If you'd done the paper the way I asked you to, I'd be graduating from UCLA and on my way to law school and engaged to Jessica. Or graduating from UCLA and on my way to law school and a queer with a whatever you want to call him. Instead of which I'm drinking coffee with you on the roof of the Uffizi." He leaned back. "I'm not saying you didn't screw things up for me. I'm just saying the jury's still out on whether it was all for the best or not. And of course I'd be a hypocrite if I pretended it was only for the paper. It was never only for the paper."

"So what are your plans?"

"Well, for now I'm studying social work at San Francisco State. My goal is to go for my master's, then work with PWAs."

"That's great."

"Oh, and also — this may surprise you — I've been trying my hand at fiction writing."

"Really."

"Well, I figured, why not? See, since I moved in with Keith, I've been reading every gay novel I can get my hands on. I even read two of yours. I liked *The Lost Language of Cranes* all right. I didn't much like *Equal Affections.*"

"I probably should have written it as a memoir. I still might."

"Interesting. As for me, I was thinking our little adventure might make a terrific story."

"That's a good idea," I said. "Writers often disguise their lives as fiction. The thing they almost never do is disguise fiction as their lives."

There wasn't really any way to answer this remark, and so for a few more moments we were both silent. Then Ben said, "And how about you, Mr. Leavitt? Do you feel comfortable with what you did?"

I spooned up the last remnants of my cappuccino foam. "Well, I'll never look at it as the proudest moment of my life, if that's what you're asking. Still, I'm not ashamed. I mean, is it wrong for the ghostwriter to say yes to the First Lady because she can't write? Was it wrong for Marni Nixon to dub Natalie Wood's voice in *West Side Story* because she couldn't sing?"

"You tell me. Was it?"

But I couldn't answer.

We got up shortly after that. It was nearing one, when Ben and Keith had a date to meet outside Café Rivoire. From the spot where Savonarola had burned the vanities, I watched them kiss each other on the cheek, two handsome, nicely dressed young men. Then, arms linked, they strolled together down Via Calzaiuoli.

And how did I feel? Ashamed, yes. Also happy. For the one thing I hadn't explained to Ben — the one thing I could never explain to Ben — was that those papers, taken together, constituted the best work I'd done in my life. And perhaps this was precisely *because* they were written to exchange for pleasure, as opposed to those tokens with which one can merely purchase pleasure. Thus the earliest troubadours sang, so that damsels might throw down ropes from virginal balconies.

Still, I couldn't have said any of this to Ben, because if I'd said any of this to Ben — if I'd told him it was the best work I'd done in my life — he would have thought it a tragedy, not a victory, and that I couldn't have borne.

From Savonarola's circle, I turned toward the Uffizi corridor, opening out like a pair of forceps. Pigeons, masses of them, circled in the sky, sometimes alighting on the heads of the statues: the imitation David, Neptune, Hercules, and Cacus, with their long fingers and outsize genitals. *And toward this nexus, great waves of men once moved,* I thought, *drawn by the David himself, by the dream of freedom itself.* It would have made a wonderful paper. . . . Meanwhile bells rang. Ben and his companion had disappeared. "Time for lunch!" called an old man with bread, and the pigeons flocked and swooped to the earth.

The Wooden Anniversary

I HADN'T SEEN CELIA IN SIX YEARS. None of her old friends had — not since she'd married Seth Rappaport and moved with him to Italy. So when I got off the train at Montesepolcro and looked around the platform for the Celia I remembered — the old Celia, fat and bewildered — the elegant woman who greeted me in her stead took me completely by surprise. And probably the expression of astonishment, even shock, in my eyes, pleased her: certainly it would have pleased me had the tables been turned; had it been Celia, fatter than ever, who'd stepped off the train, and a transformed, model-thin Lizzie waiting to greet her.

Arm in arm, we walked to her tiny, battered Fiat. It was mid-June. Above us, on its hill, Montesepolcro loomed and shimmered. Pale meadows leapt to greet it. The air had a buttery cast, as if the sun had melted and been absorbed into the fabric of the sky.

"Well, what do you think?" Celia asked, loading my bag into her trunk with a muscular arm.

"To me it looks like a vision of heaven in a painting of purgatory." (It was my first trip to Italy, and I was inclined to tourist poetry.)

Instead of answering, Celia climbed into the Fiat, making room for me on the passenger seat, which was currently occupied by a large stack of pressed shirts. That we hadn't seen each other for so long, finally, seemed an accident: after all, she'd tendered any number of invitations over the years — first to Bill and me, then after the divorce just to me — all of them encouraging a visit to the famous Podere di Montesepolcro, where she lived and out of which she ran her cooking school. And I'd always wanted, always meant, to accept. So had our friend Nathan. We'd talked about it every time we'd seen each other in New York, at parties, or in line at movies. Only Nathan was working for his father, and I was getting married; then Nathan's friend Martin was sick, and Bill was leaving me; then I was finishing up my Ph.D. (Later I got the job I have now, teaching classics at a West Side prep school.) Soon we'd canceled on Celia so many times that I think she started to despair of our ever actually showing up. Martin died. My divorce came through. Suddenly there was time — too much time — and Nathan booked tickets.

"Is he here yet?" I asked Celia now, as switching on the cranky ignition, she spirited us uphill toward the heaped stone village.

She nodded. "He arrived yesterday, and — well, frankly, Lizzie, I'm worried."

"Worried, why?" My heart clenched, remembering Martin.

But Celia waved my anxiety away. "No, no. Healthwise, he's fine. He looks fine. The trouble is that he seems — I'm not sure how to put it — desperate."

"That's par for the course," I said, relieved. "Nathan always seems desperate."

"'World-weary and travel-worn.' That's what he told me when I picked him up. 'Celia, I am world-weary and travel-worn.'"

"He's always saying things like that."

"I know. Only this time — I'm not sure why — it sounded like he meant it."

Having passed through the belt of ugly apartment buildings and shops that ringed the old center, we crossed a wooden bridge and entered Montesepolcro proper. The one street wound around and around and up and up, like a turban, then veered suddenly to the right and emerged into countryside. Cypresses lined a path that led up to Celia's farmhouse, which I recognized from photo spreads in *The New York Times, Gourmet, Travel and Leisure.*

"Wow," I said as we got out of the car. "It's even more beautiful than in the pictures."

"Thanks. But to get back to Nathan" — it seemed she still needed, perpetually, to get back to Nathan — "there's something more. He told me something strange."

"Strange in what sense?"

"It was when I picked him up at the station yesterday. He was waiting at the bar, and there was this woman at a table across the way — with a felt hat, in this heat! And when we got to the car, Nathan said, 'Celia, she had donkey ears.' 'I've heard of cauliflower ears, but never donkey ears!' I said. 'No,' he said, 'I mean literally. Brown and bristly and . . . twitchy.'"

"Really?" I was fascinated. "Well, that *would* explain the hat."

"Oh, Lizzie!" Celia's voice went raspy with disapproval. "Of course it *sounds* funny. Only he wasn't joking. 'I saw what I saw,' he said. And afterwards, at dinner — so glassy-eyed."

We had reached the old wall that surrounded the farmhouse. While Celia unlatched the gate, I ran my fingers over the mortar between the seams, and some of the mortar crumbled, coating them with chalk. I was taking things in: the arbor, enlaced with climbing roses, the mottles of shadow on the gravel ground, the profusion of flowers.

How had Celia managed it? I wondered, and felt, not for the first time, unequal to loveliness.

Across the courtyard, she fished in her pocket for keys. The house, which was very old, had over the years lost some of its shapeliness but none of its grace. Yes, perhaps its shoulders were a bit stooped, its rear end a bit saggy. Nonetheless it occupied its patch of earth with the confidence of one whose very presence has always silenced, encouraged, and redeemed. It had a roof of crumbling red and white slate, walls the color of milky coffee, many little odd-shaped windows. Its three wings, staggered and distinct, seemed not so much to be built as to recline along the slope of the garden, as if in another age a girl had lain down in a meadow, her head among violets, her feet pointed toward eternity.

"It's wonderful," I said, as stepping inside, I took in the sweep of terra-cotta floor, the comfortable, unfashionable couches, the fireplace and the bookshelves and the little drinks tables piled with old magazines. "And what a view! Spectacular."

"When you live here," Celia said, "you get used to the food. You even get used to the men. But this" — and she gestured toward the window — "this you never get used to."

I could see why. Texture, not color, defined this landscape: plowed fields might have been corduroy, green meadows moiré silk, a mown pasture a patch of dull suede shot through with silver threads. Elsewhere sunflowers were a Liberty print of sunflowers. And above it all, immense rocks, as if a child god, eons ago, had made a dribble castle of wet sand.

"It's too much to absorb," I said. "Too beautiful to believe in, or endure."

"A doom with a view, Nathan calls it."

"Where is he, by the way?"

"Still sleeping. And he went to bed at ten! That's nearly" — she checked her watch — "thirteen hours."

"Just let him rest. He's had a rough year."

"He also said, when he got here — he said, 'You, my dear, are a *tour de force.* Whereas I am forced to tour.'"

"Well, Celia, there I've got to agree with him. I mean, you put us all to shame, living in this gorgeous house, with all this success, on top of which — is it gauche of me to say anything about your weight?"

"Say it."

"Not only are you not fat, you're thin! How much have you lost, fifty pounds?"

"Seventy-five. But a fat person," she went on sternly, "in her mind at least, will always be fat. I look in the mirror even now and I see the old fat Celia, wearing bedspreads for skirts."

"That's not what I see."

"You're nice, Lizzie. You've always been nice. Nathan, on the other hand, just reminds me at every opportunity how fat I *used* to be. In so many ways, he hasn't changed!" With which remark she picked a dead bloom off an arrangement of marigolds. Obviously she and Nathan — attached, it sometimes seemed, since time immemorial — were not experiencing the easiest reentry into friendship.

Celia now led me into the kitchen, where we sat across

from each other at an old refectory table. Braids of garlic and hot peppers garlanded the iron stove. Basil grew in a pot next to the sink, while in other pots, bunches of oregano, rosemary, and sage were drying. Perhaps it is always the habit of women to need to be in a kitchen in order to speak intimately. Certainly it was our habit. So we sat there, and talked about marriage. Marriage, after all, had brought Celia to Italy. But now Seth was nowhere to be seen. They had an arrangement, she said. "I live here, and he lives in Rome. That way we get along very nicely."

"How long have you two been married now? I forget."

"Five years next week. The wooden anniversary."

"How funny! Next week would have been three years for Bill and me." I watched the play of light on the little cup she handed me. "And now you don't live together, but you stay married. Why?"

"We need each other," Celia said, pouring coffee. "There's this connection. It's hard to explain."

"Oh, I understand about that connection."

She leaned closer. "Listen, Lizzie, before we go on, there's something I've got to ask you about Nathan. I know he looks fine, but is he fine?"

My fingers closed around the handle of the cup. "I was going to ask *you* the same question."

"But I don't know! He absolutely won't talk about Martin. Instead all he does is narrate his sex adventures on the Internet."

"With me too! And it's so boring! Gay men always think—"

"*Please don't talk about me when I'm gone,*" a baritone interrupted.

We turned. All at once the object of our speculation was

standing before us, looking raffish and handsome in his half-buttoned oxford shirt, his gray hair sleep-stiff.

"Good morning, Nathan."

"Good morning, Celia. And Lizzie!"

"Hello, Nathan."

We hugged discreetly, as I knew physical intimacy with women embarrassed him, then, letting go, both smiled at Celia. She was staring at us with eyes in which wariness, affection, and rebuke forged a kind of rough and refining fire.

"Up early as usual, I see."

"It's been a long life." Grinning, he reached out his arms.

To my mild surprise, she allowed him to hug her.

That afternoon we took a walk in the hills and tried to remember how Nathan and Celia had met. We knew it was freshman year in college, probably in a dining hall; but who had introduced them? What had they talked about? Neither one could recall.

What Celia did recall was that at first Nathan had had no particular interest in her per se; rather, he had hoped, through her, to get to her friend Andrew.

"That's absolutely not true!"

"Selective memory," Celia said. In any case, seventeen years had now passed since that fateful, forgotten meeting, seventeen years over the course of which their shared lives had fragmented and become diffuse. They no longer talked to each other every day, or even every year. Still, each kept abreast of the other's doings, in no small part thanks to the efforts of their loyal friend Lizzie, always noted for her go-betweening, her faithful correspondence.

Now Nathan wanted to know how Celia had ended up

becoming such a famous chef. "After all, when I knew you, you never cooked anything except tea."

"Not a long story. We bought the house, and when we couldn't afford the renovations, Seth suggested we should turn it into a cooking school. Everyone's doing it these days. Even the Medicis."

"So did you study?"

"No, I just read cookbooks. I'm not very imaginative in the kitchen, but then again, if you want to cook good Italian food, I'm more and more convinced, you're better off *not* being imaginative. A friend of mine once said that Italian cooking is entirely about obedience."

"And are they usually women who come?" I inquired.

"Usually. Sometimes couples. Also last year a group of gay men booked for a week. Then they canceled at the last minute because one of them had to go into the hospital. When they asked if they could get their deposit back, there was a little unpleasantness from Seth."

"Too bad," Nathan said. "Nothing more entertaining than a bunch of queens in the kitchen." And clearing his throat, he mimicked: "'Derek, what on earth do you think you're doing with that sauce? Don't you know how to make a roux?' 'Of course I know how to make a roux!' 'Oh, shut up, Dolores! You'll have to excuse her, Miss Hoberman, she's on the rag today!'" His voice went high and nasal in imitation of faggotry, and he laughed. And Celia laughed too, though half-heartedly. Among the many things about Nathan that hadn't changed was his contempt for anything queeny or camp, not to mention his unconsciousness that when he aped such voices, he sounded alarmingly like himself.

"Well, in any event, I returned the deposit."

"So what do you do with these ladies all day?" I queried, to get away from death and Seth.

"Oh, it's not too difficult to keep them happy. What my brochure promises is a really authentic experience of Tuscany, and that's what I give them. They live in the house. They go shopping at the market. And of course, three or four times during the stay, Mauro takes them sightseeing. Siena, San Gimignano, Pienza —"

"Mauro?"

"My partner. A young chef from Rome."

Nathan snapped a twig in half.

"Yes," Celia continued, "I think I can fairly say that if I've got a good reputation in certain circles of New Jersey, Westchester, and Long Island synagogue society, it's due in part, at least, to Mauro."

"I will never understand the American female's appetite for unconsummated flirtation with Wops," Nathan said. "One *o sole mio* and they're . . ."

Celia glared.

"So have you eaten Mauro's cooking?" I asked Nathan. "Is it to die for?"

"Beats me. I haven't even met him."

"Mauro's been at his mother's place the last couple of days. He'll arrive here tomorrow."

"The thing about Italian men —" Nathan began. "On second thought, maybe I'd better not say."

"No, go on."

"Well, for instance, there was this Italian guy at my gym last year. He was spending a year at Columbia Business School. Fabio. Very hot, maybe twenty-eight, with one of those incredible Italian hairy chests? And one afternoon we were both changing, and he forgot to lock his locker. So naturally, good homosexual that I am, I decided to sniff his underwear —"

"Oh, Nathan!"

"Now don't act all shocked, Celia! I refuse to believe that marriage has made a prude of you. Anyway, to get back to my story, I waited until the coast was clear, and then I opened the locker and lifted Fabio's underpants out of his pants. These very European little white briefs, no fly-flap. And I lifted them up and breathed like this." He inhaled dramatically.

"And?" I asked.

"Eternity."

"God, Nathan!" Celia said.

"No, Eternity the perfume. By Calvin Klein. I nearly suffocated. Such a disappointment! Not a single healthy natural male odor. Also, I'd always noticed that his shirts were perfectly smooth. You know the reason? He pulled his shirttails all the way *through* the leg holes of his briefs."

"Yes, they all do that," Celia said, as turning off the path, she led us over a slope, into a meadow rife with timothy, dung patties, patches of wild thyme. Not far off, some brown and white cows with heavy bells around their necks lowed and chewed their cud. On the other side of the sky from the flared sun, an opalescent moon rose, Montesepolcro glimmering in its beams like a jeweled crown.

A silence fell. I had the sense of an unspoken something between Celia and Nathan, a something comprised chiefly of love, yet alloyed with anger and disapproval. And this something was acting on Celia's need like a whisk on egg whites. Which didn't surprise me: a certain degree of resentment, we all knew, had always marbled their affection for each other. So when Celia suddenly turned to Nathan, and said, "This can't go on," all that was new — all that seemed to reflect our long absence from her — was the authority that marked her tone.

Almost placidly he smiled. "What can't go on, Celia?"

"All of this. It's like we're constantly talking *around* the most important thing."

"And what would that be, pray tell?"

"Well — how you *are.*"

"How I am." He smiled. "Okay, I'll tell you. Healthwise, fine, so far as I know. Otherwise, how I am is pretty unreal."

"Unreal?"

"Like when you're a little kid, and you wonder if everything in a room disappears the instant you leave it. Did you ever wonder that?"

"No," Celia said.

"Oh, I did. All the time. In those days I doubted every reality except my own. In fact it's only lately, since Martin died, that I've felt the reverse."

We gazed at him in confusion.

"I mean, that everything's real *except* me."

"How so?" I asked.

"Well, to give you an example, a couple of weeks ago, in New York, I was leaving this bar. It was in a really seedy part of the East Village. And I noticed a woman walk by on the street, a young woman. Pretty. She was wearing a fuzzy pink bathrobe tied around her waist with one of those pink bathrobe belts, and fuzzy pink slippers, just like my mother used to have, and she was just walking, back and forth, back and forth, along this terrible street with piss on the walls and crack vials. And suddenly it occurred to me that maybe she wasn't a crack addict or street person, but someone having a dream. You know, one of those nightmares where you find yourself somewhere unexpected — school, a strange city — in your bathrobe and pajamas. And I became so convinced this woman was someone having a dream that I began to wonder whether I was a person at all, or just a figure in this woman's dream who'd disappear when she woke up. I thought it must be terrible for her, wondering where she was, why she wasn't in her bed, and I wanted to run up to her and shake her awake, so that the dream would end. But then I thought, if I do that, I might disappear too, in a cloud of smoke, as it were. And I got really scared. Terrified." He straightened his back.

"If you go, the cow stops," Celia said.

We looked at her blankly.

"*The Longest Journey.* Remember? All those Cambridge boys arguing about the reality of the cow. And I thought Forster was saying the cow only existed when we were there to perceive it, but then the professor — Crane, wasn't it? — reminded us that in England, 'stop' means 'to stay.' And you said — I remember this distinctly — you said, maybe an English cow *stays* but an American cow *ceases.*"

"Hmm," Nathan said.

"I thought you were very clever," said Celia. "But that's beside the point."

"So what is the point?"

"The point is, in Montesepolcro the cow stays. The cow is real."

"Celia, you ran out on me. In my hour of need, when Martin had just tested positive. Why?"

"I needed to be the center of someone's life."

"You were the center of my life."

"No, *you* were the center of *my* life. It's not the same thing."

"Still," Nathan said, looking away, "I was your best friend."

"And I was in love with you. Yes. I can say it now. You didn't want it to be true, you kept trying to pretend it wasn't true, but it was. Our relationship existed in a different reality from the one you tried to put it in. The cow was real. I was the cow."

"You were not a cow."

"Oh, men used to call me a cow all the time. 'You fat cow,' they'd say. And you never get used to it. Being pretty seemed pointless, since you were indifferent to women, and I was indifferent to everyone but you, and all you did was stand me up every time some juicy little boy showed up on the horizon."

"I never stood you up!"

"Selective memory!" Celia repeated. "You stood me up all the time. You just thought I didn't care. But, Nathan, what did you think I did all those nights? Just sit at home watching David Letterman? No! I sat at home and seethed." She brushed her hands on her dress. "The thing about men like you — Seth's the same way — you're terrified of mattering to people. And so when you think you've hurt someone, you bolt and run. You put the letters away unopened. You ignore the messages on the answering machine. But the fact is, I didn't disappear when you left the room, no matter how much you might have liked me to. I stayed, and I hurt."

"As I recall," Nathan said, "it was you who never answered my messages."

"Call it a preemptive strike."

Silence followed this extraordinary burst of antipathy — silence, and poetically (perhaps too poetically), a loud moo from one of the cows.

"Still, it *was* an abandonment," Nathan observed after a while, his soft voice coming too late.

"An abandonment," she answered, "for which you're punishing me now?"

He was silent. Meanwhile a breeze came up. The sun was falling like a gold coin into a child's bank.

"We'd better get back," Celia said, and turning, led us to the path, and the *podere.*

Dinner that night was a rather sullen, if delicious, affair, at the end of which we all went to bed early. Both Nathan and I were, as I have noted, jet-lagged. As for Celia — I remember this about her — ill humor tended to put her to sleep.

Before I continue, some information about the arrangement of the rooms in the farmhouse seems to me in order. On the second floor, Celia kept for herself a lavish suite consisting of a salon, a bedroom, a kitchenette, and an enormous bath. She escaped into this suite, she explained to me later, when she needed to get away from her students, or when Seth was in residence (which was rarely). Down the hall from the suite, in turn, came four largish bedrooms, each named for a different color. One of these (red, next to Celia) I occupied; the other three were uninhabitable at the moment, as their bathrooms were being renovated. Finally, on the lower level, there were three more bedrooms — two for guests and one for Mauro, which was nominal as he spent most nights with his girlfriend in Montesepolcro. Nathan's bedroom, the blue room, which was located partly beneath mine and partly beneath Celia's, shared a bathroom with Mauro's, the other downstairs room being, like the ones upstairs, in the process of refurbishment.

Of course, that first night, I knew none of this. I learned it all much later, when the sleeping arrangements started to have consequences. That first night, instead, I went to bed innocent and a little cross, only to find that in spite of being dog-tired I couldn't sleep. So I read for a while, and did the Sunday *Times* crossword puzzle, and the acrostic. Then finally — it was now past midnight — worry about how tired I'd be in the morning impelled me out of bed entirely, and needing to do *something*, I went into the bathroom and moisturized my face with some very nice Clarins cream I'd bought at the duty-free at Kennedy. The rituals of the boudoir, like those of the tea-room, have always been a source of consolation to me, a reminder that beneath the flux and bumptiousness of daily life a steadier stream does run, albeit one the music of which most men don't have the patience to listen for.

In any event, I was three-quarters of the way through this ritual when I heard, or thought I heard, the sound of gravel scraping.

I looked out the little bathroom window. A shadowy figure appeared to be pushing Celia's car down the road toward Montesepolcro: yes, pushing it, with one hand on the steering wheel and the other on the door. And who was this figure? I wondered. Was it Celia? I couldn't quite tell, though I stuck my head as far out the window as I could manage.

Finally the car went around a bend and disappeared. From a distance I heard the engine cough into life.

Well, that's odd! I thought, closing the window. Where on earth is Celia going at this hour — and why is she taking such precautions to make sure no one hears her?

If it *was* Celia. Or maybe someone was stealing her car. Yet why steal an old Fiat like that?

It was now close to one in the morning. Tired of being

tired, I resorted to half a Valium, which threw me into a deep, if uneasy, sleep from which I arose just after nine. Celia and Nathan had already finished their breakfast by the time I got down to the dining room.

"Good morning," Celia said.

"Good morning."

I looked out the window, only to see the Fiat in its accustomed place.

"Did you sleep well?" Celia asked, pouring coffee.

"Not really. Typical jet lag: first I was tired, and then I was wide awake, and then there was this noise. I wonder if you heard it."

"Celia always used to sleep with earplugs," Nathan interrupted. "Do you still sleep with earplugs?"

"Yes, actually. I never hear anything at night."

"You mean you didn't —"

Under the table Nathan kicked me.

"Didn't what?"

"Nothing, I guess. It must have been one of those weird dreams. You know, where you can't quite tell what's real. Like Nathan's story!"

"Try this apricot jam," Nathan said, thrusting a pot in my direction. "Celia put it up herself."

"I'll get some more bread." Pushing out her chair, which scraped horribly against the tiles, she strode into the kitchen.

Ssh, Nathan gestured.

"All right," I whispered.

She came back in with a very clever bread board, slats of olive wood through which the crumbs fell into a tray.

"So Celia's just been telling me about her plans for the day," Nathan announced, and launched into a recitation of food and itineraries that successfully distracted all three of us from the subject of the noise.

When he'd finished, she got up and started clearing the dishes.

"I'll help," I said, almost automatically.

Nathan stayed put.

"Typical," Celia muttered.

She loaded the dishwasher. Then she said, "Well, gotta go." As it happened, she had a date to go to the market with Mauro, who was hoping to take advantage of our visit to try out some new recipes. "That is, if you two don't mind being guinea pigs."

"Mind? Why should we mind?" I asked as we followed her into the yard.

"Especially if Mauro's the great cook you claim," Nathan added.

"I don't think you'll be disappointed. Well, bye."

She drove off.

Nathan turned to me. "Thank you," he said.

"Nathan, what on earth is going on?"

"I owe you a favor, Lizzie. You covered for me."

"Did *you* take Celia's car last night?"

He nodded.

"But why all this secrecy?"

"I didn't ask her permission."

"Oh!" I laughed. "Well, at least *I'm* not hallucinating."

Nathan took the barb without flinching. "I hoped no one would hear me. I was counting on Celia's earplugs — and your being asleep."

"I wasn't."

"And I was careful. I drove very carefully."

"Nathan, you don't have to justify yourself to *me.* It wasn't my car."

"How would you have felt if it was?"

I thought about it. "Perplexed. Maybe angry. But that's beside the point, because I'm not Celia."

"Still, I want to tell you *why* I took her car, Lizzie! And what happened. In fact, I probably have to tell you, in case . . ."

"In case what?"

He sat down on a little wrought-iron bench. I sat next to him.

"First of all," he said, "you have to promise me to keep this to yourself."

"Of course."

"And you also have to promise not to tell me I'm a heel. I know I'm a heel. I don't need reproaches."

"No problem."

"All right, then." And he told me this story:

It seemed that last night Nathan, too, had gone to bed feeling out of sorts — this despite the fact that the room in which Celia had put him he found comforting. The old beams, the slanted ceiling, the bleach-colored couch and the armoire and the writing table, all spoke of permanence and occupation, he said. All invited the hanging of rumpled clothes, the setting out of pens and paper. The room might have been van Gogh's at Arles, except that the walls were bare, Nathan having carefully removed, in deference to his Jewish upbringing, the small Madonna from its nail over the bed.

Like me, he tried, and failed, to sleep. So he switched on the reading light and, climbing out of the bed, looked at his travel alarm clock. Twenty past twelve: early, by New York standards. A mad idea entered his head. In Florence, where he'd stayed a couple of nights before coming to Montesepolcro, there was an appealing stretch of park alongside the Arno to which great numbers of men flocked regularly for sex. The fresh memory of that park now stirred him. Why not go tonight? he asked himself. But no, it was impossible, Florence was miles from Montesepolcro; besides which he had no car.

But Celia has a car, a voice in his head interrupted. And the mad idea — the criminal idea — took hold.

He pulled on some clothes, then tiptoeing into the bathroom, brushed his teeth and washed his face. The toilet flushed loudly, which made him wince. He didn't want to wake Celia. Worse, it refilled itself loudly, like a thirsty dog lapping water. Still, he reasoned, if the flush woke her, the refilling might at least muffle his steps as he went down the stairs.

In the kitchen, he switched on the light. He had expected to have to search for Celia's keys, but she'd left them on the countertop, and, removing from the chain one sheathed in black plastic, he stepped quietly out the door. Here the air was still and carried the smell of jasmine. Nathan was careful to tread softly as he made his way down the gravel driveway. Then, getting into the Fiat, he put it into neutral and pushed it along the road until the house was no longer visible. Only once he thought himself out of earshot did he turn the key in the ignition. The engine stirred, and he took off, retracing the route Celia had led him along two days before, through the hole in the town wall, along the winding folds of the turban, over the wooden bridge and down the hill and past the station. Here, miraculously, a sign occurred that said FIRENZE. Within moments he was on a clear, open road.

Tavarnelle . . . San Donato . . . San Casciano. . . . On Celia's odometer, the kilometers collected. Nathan only hoped she wouldn't notice the difference in the numbers. In any case he drove fast, and as there was little traffic, found himself entering Florence around one-thirty. His good sense of direction enabled him to locate the Cascine without much trouble.

Pleased with himself, he stepped out of the car and walked. The moon was high. Beyond the long, thin stretch of parkland the river glimmered dully. It was a warm night, a kindly night, so much so that even the transsexual prostitutes plying their trade along the Viale seemed to him swathed in innocence.

Meanwhile the trees rustled in the wind, and men rustled in the trees.

He turned off the Viale and entered a wooded enclave in which the tidiness of city planning — tree, bench, tree, bench — did not obviate a certain wildness. This was because of the bats. They were everywhere, swarming the riverbanks, swooping over the water that seemed itself filled with trees: a second park, subaqueous, through which, if he dove, Nathan might stroll upside down. Cicadas played themselves, and as his eyes adjusted, the shadows coagulated into men and boys, some sitting on benches, others chatting in gangs, or attached to trees. Finding a tree that was unoccupied, Nathan assumed his standard position for this sort of enterprise: legs parted, one hand hooked through the belt loop of his jeans, the other resting on his hip, which was thrust slightly forward.

Thus he arranged himself, and opening his eyes wide, stared out into the involving dark.

A boy leaning against a tree opposite stared back.

Nathan spread his legs wider.

What an extraordinarily comfortable tree! he found himself thinking. It seemed to have been constructed specifically to accommodate the contours of his body: a Birkenstock of trees. It seemed to hold him. He thought he could feel fingers of bark working the small of his back, and wondered at the mind's capacity for tactile hallucination.

The shadowy boy now departed from his own tree, cutting a path just south of Nathan. They stared at each other as he passed. Yet the dark was vexing; he could not get a good enough look at the boy to decide whether he was attractive.

Next the boy turned around, retraced his steps, assumed, as if for no particular reason, his habitual stance — but this time next to Nathan.

"*Ciao,*" he said.

"*Ciao,*" Nathan answered.

Silence. The boy had dark hair and fair skin. His thin white T-shirt delineated perfectly the hollows and hills of his chest.

Nathan didn't need to look at him: even from a distance he could feel the waves of anxiety that radiated from the boy's body, he could feel, as if it were his own pulse, the thumping of the young heart.

He untucked and reached under the boy's T-shirt. The boy took in his breath; his abdomen heaved. Nathan pretended to pay no attention. With his eyes he scanned the other men in the area, while his hand, inevitable, continued its upward journey, resting finally on the boy's chest and working, with the laconic ease of ownership, first one and then another small nipple. Then all at once Catholic oppression gave way, and the boy embraced Nathan, pawing his chest, planting his mouth on his cheek, reaching under his shirt and grabbing hold of muscle and fat and hair. But he had no delicacy; he was a sexual pantomime; he twisted Nathan's nipples only because Nathan had twisted his. A neophyte, then. And how tired Nathan was of initiating neophytes! It seemed inevitably to be boys like this who gravitated toward him, never men his own size or age . . .

At that moment the tree spoke.

Nathan froze.

It spoke. Its voice was river reeds in a breeze.

"*Cosa?*" asked the boy.

"Ssh," Nathan said. "Listen . . ."

"*Polizia?*"

"No, no . . . a voice . . ."

"*Non capisco.*"

"Ssh."

They remained still. Once again the boy twisted Nathan's nipples. Nathan shooed him away. Removing his hand, the boy retucked his T-shirt and, with an insolent "*Ciao,*" strode off. Nathan hardly noticed. For the voice had returned, vague, caressing.

Then all at once two branches descended and twined around Nathan's chest.

Panic is instantaneous. It considers neither consequences nor impossibilities, only the quickest way to safety. And panic told Nathan to get the hell away from that tree. So he tried to step forward, but the branches tightened over him, blocking his way, and when he pushed, they tightened more, squeezing the air from his lungs. He would have screamed, but he had no breath, all he could do was push, with both fists, even as the tree struggled to keep hold of him.

The tree seemed to him to be collapsing with effort, and yet taking him in. He could feel bark crawling over his skin, into his pants. He could taste bark in his mouth.

He knew only to push blindly, mightily, to take advantage of what he perceived as the tree's momentary exhaustion.

Then he was away, torn branches in his hand.

A howl filled the air, and subsided. Nathan turned. The tree was at a distance. An ordinary tree. He was on his knees, on the ground. He could not get enough air, he was gulping huge mouthfuls of air. Meanwhile all around him men were hurrying away, for he had made a commotion, and such a delicate atmosphere as that of the Cascine at two in the morning fractures easily.

Still he could not catch his breath.

A fan of bats swooped over the river. He wanted only to get out of there, so he stumbled back to the car, got the key into the ignition, and drove off. But his hands were shaking, and, fearful lest he might stray into the opposite lane, he pulled into a twenty-four-hour gas station. Parking the car, he sat back, closed his eyes, counted his breaths until they were once again steady, even. Next he went into the bathroom, and was standing in front of the sink, wetting his hands, when he looked in the mirror and saw that his shirt was streaked with blood.

He pulled off the shirt, looked at himself once again in the mirror. Not a scratch.

Not blood, then. Juice from some sort of berry. Something smeared against something . . . tomatoes . . . someone else's blood . . .

Thrusting his shirt under the tap he rinsed it furiously until the stains faded to a soft pink. Then he stuffed it into a garbage can, and, shirtless, got back into Celia's car.

All the way to the autostrada exit he wondered if he was going mad, and by the time he drove into Montesepolcro he was sure of it. Then, as he approached Celia's house, he realized that he could not be mad because of the shirt.

The shirt he had thrown away.

Was he dreaming? He must be dreaming, he decided, and remembering how once, when he was a child, his mother had answered the question "How do I know when I'm dreaming?" by telling him to pinch himself, he pinched himself, and it hurt, so he supposed he must not be.

At Celia's, nothing seemed to have changed in his absence. The farmhouse breathed in sleep. Below him, in the darkened valley, a train glided by. It looked like a pale stream of moving light.

Stepping quietly into the arbor, he checked his watch: three o'clock. He could still manage five or six hours sleep, though it would be thin, meager. Anyway, perhaps the morning would bring with it a sense of resolution.

Then he reached for the kitchen door, and discovered that it was locked.

In his pocket, only the one key, the car key —

For a few seconds he rattled the handle, as if this would make any difference — then circled the house and tried the front door. It too was locked.

He closed his eyes, leaned his forehead against the cool stone wall, tried to cry, and, failing in the effort, walked back to the arbor and lay down, in despair, on a chaise longue. Remember that he was shirtless, and that the night was full of mosquitoes. Recognizing his vulnerability, he reached for a towel that Celia had left out, covered his chest with it, and contemplated his options. He could wake Celia; to do so, however, would be to risk her finding out that he had taken her car, and he wasn't a good liar. Alternately he might sleep in the chaise longue, and let her discover him in the morning. When she asked him what he was doing there, he could claim he'd gotten up early to take a walk and been locked out. But then how to explain the mosquito bites with which he would no doubt be covered, not to mention the absence of his shirt? And more fundamentally, how to persuade Celia, who knew him better than anyone in the world, that he — a notorious late riser — had done something so unlikely as get up at dawn to take a shirtless walk?

No, he decided, better just to face the music, ring the bell, bow before his friend in her justifiable wrath, and hope, as he had hoped so many times before, that she might show some mercy on him. And yet, might he not stand a better chance with her in the morning? No doubt a Celia refreshed from a night of sleep would be more compassionate than a Celia roused rudely from her slumber.

Anyway, the borscht belt comedian in him observed, it could be worse. It could be raining.

This was the cue for rain to begin, but it didn't. Again, he closed his eyes. He didn't want to worry about the morning, or think about the tree, or contemplate the not thrilling prospect of his own return, two weeks hence, to New York. Still, in his memory the taste of bark lingered.

Eventually he dropped off. Yet the sleep into which he fell was too tenuous to keep out the sounds and changing light, nor was it sufficiently deep to muffle his consciousness of the passage of time, a consciousness in the shadow of which time progressed with agonizing slowness. Nor was this sleep uninterrupted; indeed, the slightest disturbance jolted him out of it, and into a grim awareness not only of his dilemma, but of the dilemma that was his entire life.

Finally dawn broke. It seemed to wander up from the bottom of the world, and the light, which every day is reborn without memory, called in its nascent innocence to some nascent innocence in Nathan, making him believe that wounds could be forgiven, slates cleaned, time turned back. Possibilities danced before his eyes, possibilities that he knew, in a few hours, the grim brilliance of high noon would desiccate. Yet for the moment they were alive.

And then, in an instant, two brindle-and-white-spotted dogs were licking his arms, compelling him to open his eyes, to sit up, to pat first one, then another soft, spotted head.

"Nice doggie," he murmured. "You're a good doggie, aren't you?" A hummingbird flew within inches of his face.

He looked up and saw standing before him a tall young man, shirtless like himself, his mostly hairless chest gleaming in the early light, the pale skin flushed with vitality, as if it had been recently handled. This young man wore on his face an expression somewhere between guardedness and delight. There emanated from his body the smell of lemons. He smiled crookedly. Altogether he presented an impression of extraordinary but unlikely beauty which the fact that he was slightly cross-eyed only heightened. Indeed, he might have been one of Bronzino's cavaliers, divested, for the moment, of his brocades and codpiece; a knight who had taken a bath in the woods, or spent an hour sporting with a maiden.

"Luna, Venta, *venite!*" the young man called then, and the spaniels went to him. Awkwardly Nathan sat up. The towel fell from his chest, so that he wondered whether to pick it up again.

The young man asked something complicated in Italian.

"*Scusa?*"

"Ah, you're American" — this time in good English. "You must be one of Celia's visitors."

"Yes, I'm Nathan."

"I'm Mauro." The hand which he reached down yanked Nathan to his feet.

"The chef!"

"*Chef!* I hate these French words. *Cook* is quite fine. And you? Did Celia compel you for some reason to sleep outside?"

"I got locked out," Nathan said, and looked at his watch. "Six-thirty! Do you always get here so early?"

"Not usually," Mauro said. "Only I was sleeping last night at my girlfriend's house in Montesepolcro . . . Well, I suppose you would like to go back inside."

"You have a key?"

"Of course!"

With that Mauro strode over to the kitchen door, and taking a chainful of keys from his pocket, unlocked it.

"I'll make coffee," he said, as they stepped through, then reaching into a high cabinet, chose some beans for grinding. He hadn't bothered to put on his shirt again, and Nathan, admiring the corded muscles of Mauro's back, lamented his own nakedness. After all, he had always been the sort who looks better in clothes.

"I think I'll take a shower," he said next, and surreptitiously slipped the car key back onto Celia's key ring.

"*Bene,*" Mauro said, pouring milk into a saucepan. "And when you get back, maybe you ought to tell me what happened — in case I have to lie for you."

He flashed Nathan a brilliant smile. There was no calculation in it, only good humor and a little shyness.

"Yes, of course," Nathan said, "of course I will," and went off, amid the coffee smells, to take his shower.

Later, of course, I would grow more articulate; I would have ideas of my own. That morning, however, as Nathan finished telling me his story, I found myself literally at a loss for words. What could I say to him, after all, when my own experience of the "supernatural" was limited to a single encounter with an apparent poltergeist that had once broken some of my mother's best china? In that case, the poltergeist had turned out to be my brother Eddie, who had drug problems; nonetheless I hesitated to offer the example to Nathan, for fear that it would seem I was trying to rationalize away what had happened to him. Which I didn't want to do. On the contrary, I felt that I owed it to him to accept his account at face value: in all its singularity and antique terror.

Nathan, on the other hand, appeared not to believe himself, or at least to be disappointed by my credulity.

"Well, who's to say I *wasn't* hallucinating?" he asked.

"Do you think you were hallucinating?"

He considered for a moment. "No. Then again if I really am psychotic, I'm hardly in a position to assess the parameters of my own psychosis, right?"

"Maybe. Or maybe something really did happen."

"Is that supposed to comfort me?"

"Doesn't it?"

"No! Decidedly not!"

"Why?"

"Because if it wasn't real, I'm just another human being going mad. Whereas if it was real, then the world's going mad. And something else may happen."

"Yes, I see your point." We were quiet for a moment.

"Anyway," he concluded, "at least now you know. So if I disappear tomorrow, don't assume I've gone somewhere. Talk to trees."

Since there didn't seem much I could say to that, we went into the kitchen and drank some blood orange juice from a carton in the refrigerator. Celia came home. "Hi, guys," she said, her arms full of onions. "Gosh, have you two been sitting here reminiscing this whole time?"

"Sort of." Rather awkwardly, we smiled. Meanwhile, just outside the door, Mauro waited. I thought his eyes met Nathan's uneasily before he crossed the threshold and, reaching out his hand, introduced himself.

Now: a word about Mauro. There was no denying that he was good-looking. Not that I would have likened Nathan's rescuer, as he had, to a Bronzino knight; his self-presentation was entirely too modern for that. Still, the fact cannot be ignored that in certain Italian faces that aristocratic sullenness that animates Renaissance portraiture does linger. And in Mauro — how else to put it? — blood told. Yes, blood told, and it was in his ankles, brown and elegant in Top-Siders, that curiously enough, it told the most.

After we'd finished lunch, the four of us walked into Montesepolcro to have a coffee at the Bar Garibaldi. Tourism is correct in noting that in every little town in Tuscany there is a Bar Garibaldi, or a Bar Centrale, or a Bar Italia — to which observation I shall add only that in this particular Bar Garibaldi, a red-haired boy was arranging coconut wedges on a three-tiered revolving tray; listlessly, the tray revolved; listlessly, listlessly trickles of water poured from a spout at its tip, ostensibly to moisten the coconut, but really, I think, in feeble imitation of those glorious fountains that in Renaissance water gardens jet upward before spilling over artful arrangements of carved stone. Or so mused my imagination that afternoon, an imagination still radiant with that amazement that so often marks the visitor's first days in Italy. And you cannot feel it twice. It is like the pleasure that accompanies the first reading of a great novel, something that can afterward be approximated, but never replicated, so that no matter how many fond returns you make, no matter how many coconut trays you see, you must always envy the virgin eyes of the neophyte.

But to get back to the story: as is the habit among Italians, we took our coffees standing up. Mauro and Nathan, I noticed, were pretending they'd only just met each other, a somewhat theatrical bit of dissimulation in the enactment of which Nathan's spirits seemed to rally considerably. I'd never deny that he's the sort of person in whom deviousness always provokes a little thrill. As for Celia, I didn't know if she had a clue as to what had taken place during the night; if so, she certainly didn't let it on. Instead she drank her coffee placidly. Perhaps she too was dissimulating; especially now, I wonder. Or perhaps she simply hadn't noticed the numbers on her odometer.

So there we were at the Bar Garibaldi, and Mauro was telling Nathan the history of the dish he and Celia intended to prepare for supper that evening. "It is called *La Genovese,*" he said, "even though it is Neapolitan, because the Genovese used to own a lot of trattorias in Naples —"

"Basically it's a pot roast made with about five kilos of onions," Celia said. "And cooked for hours. First you eat the *sugo* — all melty onions and white wine and beef drippings — with the pasta —"

"Pasta *lisce,* not pasta *rigate.*"

"And then you have the meat as the *secondo.*"

"It sounds delicious," I said.

"Your English is very good, Mauro," Nathan said. "Where did you learn it?"

"Mauro studied two years at the University of Minnesota."

"Also, my mother was half-American. I've spent several summers with my relatives in Milwaukee."

"Ah, that explains it. And does Roman cooking go down well in Milwaukee?"

"As long as I don't use too much *peperoncino*."

"As far as I'm concerned," Celia said, "there's no such thing as too much *peperoncino*."

"Yes, I remember that about you," Nathan said. "At this Greek pizza place we used to go to," he said to Mauro, "Celia liked to shake so much hot pepper onto her pizza that if she got some on her fingers and rubbed her eyes — and she was always rubbing her eyes — they'd swell up and tear."

"A *Greek* pizza place? How strange. To me Celia does not talk so much about her college days."

"Oh, but there are such stories to tell! Celia, don't you have any old pictures lying around?"

"All burned." Celia drained her coffee. "Well, shall we head back home and start chopping onions?" And we headed back home and started chopping onions: all four of us in the kitchen, chopping, chopping. And what a difference, I observed, between Mauro's face, with its flustered vivacity, and my ex-husband Bill's face, getting jowly as he neared forty, and Nathan's face, to the middle-aged contours of which his never-changing repertoire of boyish expressions now lent a comical, even clownish aspect! Poor Nathan. He did not fare well in the comparison. For Mauro, though no older than twenty-seven or twenty-eight, clearly felt comfortable being a man; indeed, had probably felt comfortable being a man even before he was one. Whereas Nathan seemed logjammed in a sort of perpetual adolescence, and where his features were becoming every day more masculine and rugged, the spirit that animated them remained that of an aggravated, even aggrieved childhood: a childhood that had lasted too long.

Onions, onions. My eyes started to tear. Meanwhile across the room Mauro was describing to Nathan the red wine he had just brought up from the *cantina.* "It comes from near Ancona, and tastes like violets," he said, then went on to explain certain technical aspects of its character — tannins and such — of the sort upon which heterosexual men (my husband was the same way) seem always to dote so fondly; and this knowledge, curiously, Nathan, whom details usually bored, lapped up as thirstily as if it were the wine itself.

"Mauro, why don't you take Nathan to that *enoteca* in Siena?" Celia suggested. "He might get a kick out of it."

"Would you like to go?" Mauro asked.

"I'd love to."

And so, soon enough, the *Genovese* was bubbling on the stove, and Mauro and Nathan were on their way to the *enoteca* in Siena, leaving Celia and me to girl talk and a little messing around in the vegetable garden.

"Tell me more about Mauro," I said to her when we were alone, and she was picking leaves of bitter chicory for the evening salad.

"Not much to tell, really. He's a sweet boy."

"Gorgeous, if you want my opinion."

She looked up from her lettuces. "What, are you interested in him, Lizzie?" she asked, her voice a little sharp.

"He has a girlfriend, doesn't he?"

"How did you know? Did he tell you?"

"Well, I just assumed. A good-looking boy like that."

Celia returned to her chicory. "No, of course he has a girlfriend. In fact, that's how I managed to get him to work for me. You see, before I hired him, he cooked at this trattoria in Rome where Seth and I used to eat all the time — a wonderful place — and one evening the three of us got to talking, and he mentioned the girlfriend. She was from Montesepolcro, and he was looking for a job in the area."

"What a coincidence!"

"A match made in heaven, you might say."

"I hope they don't break up. Wouldn't he go back to his Roman trattoria?"

"Maybe. I don't know. I think he likes it up here. He sleeps every night at her house," she added. "Very Italian. Sneaks in after the parents have gone to bed. They pretend they don't know."

Her basket was now so full that leaves were dropping over the edge. "Ah, Celia," I said, for I was feeling moony, "maybe a boy like that would be the answer to all my troubles. Do you think so? Well-mannered, easy on the eyes. After Bill, I've had enough complicated Americans."

"But Italian men aren't so simple as everybody thinks."

"Oh, I realize —"

"They're vain and smug and think they're little gods because of their mothers. Which doesn't mean they don't have a certain appeal. I'd *never* deny that. Still, let's be realistic. How could you make a life with a boy like Mauro? You wouldn't have anything to talk about except food."

"Well, who says we'd have to talk?"

"Oscar Wilde said that conversation has to be the basis of any marriage."

"Oscar Wilde is like Freud. Everyone thinks that just because he said something, it's automatically true."

"But isn't it in this case? And anyway, conversation's important. For instance, Seth and I, the one thing we really do have going for us is conversation. We talk all the time on the phone, about books and music, America and Italy. I couldn't give that up."

I wondered why she said this. Had someone asked her to give it up?

"Well, I gave it up, and I must say, I feel a whole lot better. Not that I don't see your point," I continued. "But a vacation romance with a handsome Italian — I could get into that, Celia." I poked her in the ribs. "Mauro doesn't happen to have a brother, does he?"

"Three. Two married and one ten."

"Just my luck."

We returned to the kitchen, where Celia washed the salad, leaving it to dry on a dishcloth. Then she joined me at the table. "Lizzie, now that we're alone," she said, "I *would* like to talk to you a little more about Nathan."

Of course, I thought. In his presence, Celia always seemed irritated with Nathan, whereas when we were by ourselves, her tone became conciliatory, even maternal.

"Go on."

"Well, first of all, you know that he and I have always had a very complicated relationship. I was in love with him, and so whenever he treated me like a sister, I resented it. I still do."

"As much?"

"Less. I've grown up, I suppose. Still, there's an anxiety. And also, naturally, I worry about him. What does his future hold?"

"I find it hard to worry *too* much about someone who's as rich as Nathan is," I observed practically.

"Oh, I know that. And yet, don't you wonder sometimes what's going to become of him, money aside? No career to speak of. Also, the whole time we've known each other, except for Martin, he's never had a long-term boyfriend. And God knows he isn't getting any younger, Lizzie."

"Well, maybe he's the sort of person who's happiest single."

She played with her wedding ring. "I guess the thing that surprises me is that after six years, his wants haven't changed. Nothing's changed. He shows up, and he's demanding, insensitive. Like the other day when I picked him up at the station. Automatically *I* carried his bags to the car. And he didn't even try to stop me!"

"But that's just the kick-me sign, Celia!"

"The what?"

"You know, kid comes up to smaller kid, pretends to pat him on the back but actually tapes a sign to his back that says 'kick me.' Then all the other kids kick him, until some adult notices."

"And you're saying there's a kick-me sign on my back?"

"Nathan may find it hard to resist."

Celia seemed to think about this for a moment. Then she said, "Well, if that's the case, if I'm wearing, as you say, a kick-me sign, it was Nathan who put it there. He put it there seventeen years ago, the first time he ever came to my dorm room."

"Does that mean only he can take it off?"

"Oh no. I've already taken it off myself."

"Have you?"

Getting up, she nibbled a piece of lettuce.

"Well, anyway," I went on, "my main point is, I wouldn't worry too much. For instance, if Nathan were really losing it, somehow I doubt he'd have taken such an interest in wine — or Mauro."

Celia crossed her arms. "Oh, he'll never get anywhere with Mauro. Mauro's invincibly heterosexual."

"A challenge, then?"

"One he'll never meet."

She pulled a dead leaf off her basil plant.

"You know what my problem is?" she said then. "My life is composed too much of food. You can't imagine. This week is an exception. Usually it's just American women, and cooking, and cooking. So much cooking it loses all relationship to eating. And you have to stay hungry all the time, Lizzie: you can't cook when you're full. That's how I lost the weight. And soon everything you see starts to be food. The grass looks like spaghetti. Shells on the beach are pasta shells. And the smell! That little odor of onion, all the time, on your fingertips." She shook her head. "I never meant to be a cook. Mauro, he's a natural. He has an instinct for these things. But me, I'm just a slave to instruction."

"Oh, I doubt that —"

"All I wanted was to live here, in this house, this countryside. That was the only reason I got into the business, so that we could have quiet, and a place for Seth to work on his translations."

"But he's never here."

"Oh, sometimes he'll come up for a few days. But then there's too much noise, or one of the clients asks him to mix her a drink, or fix the window in her room, like he's the bellhop or something. And he hates that. At most he'll last forty-eight hours before heading back to Rome."

"Do you mind?"

She shrugged. "I'm pretty indifferent, to tell the truth. When we're together, we bicker. Whereas on the phone, we have the most fantastic conversations. Very nineties, that. If we keep going in this direction, pretty soon our whole relationship will be E-mail."

Moving toward the stove, she opened the lid of the *Genovese.* From underneath a heady fog pulsed out, steaming my glasses, which I had to wipe with a napkin. "Basil," Celia said, tasting, and, pinching a few leaves off the plant that bloomed on her windowsill, tore them into the *sugo.* And how luxurious that plant seemed to me then — effulgent, even excessive — as if Celia, like Boccaccio's Isabella, had buried a lover's head in the soil, then watered it with her tears.

She stirred, tasted again, pinched in some salt.

"What do you mean you don't have instincts?"

"Oh, Mauro never has to taste anything. He just knows."

"Handsome, and a cook. All the more reason for me to grab him up."

"Oh, Lizzie!" She wagged a finger at me. "My God, all he reads is *Il Corriere dello Sport.*"

"Sounds wonderful."

Ignoring me, she replaced the lid.

After that, for a week or so, life got so busy that I lost touch with the dramas and melodramas attendant on Celia and Nathan's reunion. Instead, under Mauro's guidance (or so it seemed to me), activity consumed us. He took us to the cathedral in Siena, the church of Santa Fina in San Gimignano (which Forster reinvented as the church of Santa Deodata in *Where Angels Fear to Tread*), the water gardens at the Villa Lante. And Celia, in her dark glasses, seemed easy on these expeditions. So did Nathan, who shopped for alabaster eggs and other *prodotti tipici* with all the hell-bent alacrity of a Jewish aunt on a Perillo tour. Likewise he took pictures with hell-bent alacrity: it seemed we were forever being posed and grouped in front of monuments, or against the backdrop of stirring views. Especially Mauro. The rapid evolution of their friendship, on which Celia never remarked, certainly raised my eyebrows. Might it have taken on an erotic cast? I couldn't help but wonder, all the while reproaching myself for such suspiciousness. After all, there was the matter of that unseen girlfriend, to whose Montesepolcro balcony, like Romeo, he repaired every midnight, no doubt by means of a rope or a secreted ladder. And anyway, if Mauro and Nathan were, as it appeared, just friends, such a friendship would probably be better than a love affair for Nathan, who had started doing things under Mauro's aegis which he'd never done in all the years we'd known him. One afternoon, for instance, Celia and I looked out the kitchen window and saw that on the lawn, Mauro was teaching Nathan — Nathan! — the rudiments of soccer. Hidden by gardenias, we giggled as they kicked the ball around — Mauro graceful and lithe in shorts and jersey, Nathan lumbering and scoliotic in jeans and sweatshirt. Like a lynx playing soccer with an octopus, Celia said, and I laughed; we were that glad. And judging from his smile, Nathan was glad too, which made us remember the story he used to tell about the elementary school teacher who wrote on his report card, "Though Nathan isn't as well coordinated as the other children, he certainly does enjoy himself at games." It was good, I supposed, to see him enjoying himself again.

One morning — it was now a little more than a week into our visit — Celia announced yet another expedition: she and Mauro were going to take us to see the Olivone, the oldest olive tree in the world. And since this natural wonder was located relatively far from Montesepolcro, more than an hour's drive, it had been decided that we should go in two cars, Mauro's Alfa-Romeo and Celia's Fiat, in order to spare Nathan and me the discomfort of sharing a cramped backseat.

It is a moment not unworthy of contemplation, that awkward preamble to a journey when a group of travelers, heading off in several cars, must decide who will ride with whom. Suddenly, as if out of nowhere, the emotional temperature rises. Will Nathan ride with Celia, his host, or with Mauro, his new friend? And what about Lizzie? Which driver would *she* prefer to accompany? And who would prefer to accompany her?

When the confusion finally resolved itself, it was in a surprising way: that is to say, Celia went off with Mauro in his Alfa, leaving Nathan and me to the Fiat.

He drove. As it happened, I didn't mind. I'd been hoping for an opportunity to spend a little time alone with him — this despite the fact that he was making no effort to hide his disappointment at the way the arrangements had worked out. Again, typical Nathan, not to bother to pretend.

"So," I said eventually, to break the silence. "The oldest olive tree in the world."

He murmured an assent.

"Are you scared?"

"Why should I be?"

"Well, after your encounter in Florence —"

"Oh, that." He brushed the beard buds on the underside of his chin. "My encounter, as you call it, I'm now fully convinced was a hallucination induced by jet lag. Or at least Mauro thinks so, and I'm inclined to trust him."

"Oh, you told him?"

"I had to! After all, he rescued me."

"And why does he think it was a hallucination?"

"Because something similar happened to him once. He saw a dog fall into a canal in Venice, and when it climbed out of the water, it had webbed paws, like a duck."

"Really?"

"No, *not* really. That's the point. When he saw it, he'd just finished one of those huge exams Italian students always seem to be taking. And before the exam, he hadn't slept in three days."

We had reached the autostrada. Here a tiny, rusted sign, pointing back the way we'd come, read "Montesepolcro, 4 km." Ahead of us, in the Alfa, Mauro shifted gears and, as if intent on proving the car's powers of acceleration, shot off into the distance and the future.

"How am I supposed to follow him?" Nathan asked, his voice oddly frantic. "This car won't go more than eighty."

"Don't worry. I have directions."

We merged onto the highway. Nathan drove cautiously, like an American. Periodically a little dot of light appeared in his rearview mirror, then magnified, in a matter of seconds, into the sharklike visage of a Mercedes or BMW which, having consumed the entire dimension of the mirror, flashed dangerous, impatient lights at us, as if to say, Move to the other lane or I shall with great pleasure squash your little insect of a car into pulp. These vehicular predators were usually driven by fat men talking on cellular phones. Sometimes there were beautiful women in dark glasses in the passenger seats.

As for Mauro, to my surprise, he didn't lose us. Instead he sped up and slowed down, sped up and slowed down, so that after a while it seemed he was always awaiting us over the next hill, his Alfa athrob with virile impatience.

"I'm glad to see you and Mauro have gotten to be such good friends," I said after a few kilometers.

Nathan nodded. "I only hope Celia isn't jealous."

"Why should she be?"

"Because I came to see her, and instead the person I'm

bonding with, if you'll pardon that awful word, is Mauro."

"Well, if she's jealous, she certainly hasn't mentioned it to me. To be honest, I think she's pretty preoccupied right now with her own problems."

"You mean Seth?"

"Uh-huh."

"Oh, I know," Nathan said, shaking his head. "It really is too bad about the girlfriend."

"Girlfriend? What girlfriend?"

Not very convincingly, he clapped a hand over his mouth. "You mean Celia didn't —"

"No. She only said that she and Seth don't really live together anymore."

"Oh, fuck. Then I really have let the cat out of the bag, haven't I?"

"I can't say I'm surprised to hear it."

"No, neither was I. Well, I might as well tell you the rest, since I've told you this much — only please, not a word to Celia. She doesn't know we know."

"Okay," I said, wondering why it was that in Nathan's company, one was always being pledged to keep secrets one hadn't asked to be let in on in the first place.

The secret, as it turned out, wasn't much different from what I'd guessed. According to Mauro, the real reason Seth lived in Rome was that he was having an affair with a woman there, the editor in chief of a Communist newspaper. "And Celia knows all about it," Nathan said. "Knows, and claims to accept it. Apparently — Mauro couldn't believe this — she even let him bring the girlfriend up one weekend, and gave them the best bedroom, and made them breakfast."

"Oh, Celia."

"Mauro doesn't approve," Nathan added reverently. "Mauro is a *gentiluomo*. A *cortigiano*."

"You mean like Castiglione?"

"Exactly. He holds to the old values. Loyalty, fidelity. Above all courtesy. Fuck you back!" he shouted at a Mercedes in the process of passing us. "That's why he loathes Seth. He thinks he's discourteous."

"Because of the woman."

"Also because he has no table manners, and talks too loudly, and once ate a hundred grams of this very expensive ham — *culatello,* it's called — that Mauro was saving to use in a big Easter *timballo.* Mauro just opened the refrigerator, and it was gone."

"I envy Mauro's girlfriend," I said. "The world needs more gentlemen."

"Yes, she's very lucky."

"What's her name, by the way?"

"Angela."

"And have you met her?"

Nathan shook his head. "Celia has, though. She says she's very pretty, and very shy."

Having reached the end of the autostrada, we now trailed Mauro and Celia onto a narrow two-lane road that wound through treeless hills. The plowed fields seemed upholstered in variegated shades of beige velvet. "So beautiful," I said for the thousandth time, and for the thousandth time Nathan answered "Yes." You see, we were not so much acknowledging beauty as our shared incapacity to absorb it, to feel included or involved by it as Celia seemed to feel included and involved by it. For the hard truth, growing harder as departure neared, was that we would never be of this place. Our home was elsewhere.

Though eventually we might take in the landscape, it would never take us in.

We drove silently for a few minutes. Then Nathan said, "About Mauro, do you think . . . I mean, if you can see, then maybe Celia can too, and she just isn't saying anything."

"See what?" I asked.

He paused for a moment. "That I'm in love with him."

"Ah."

"Are you shocked, Lizzie?"

"No."

"I didn't think so. I've never fallen in love this hard in my life," he added informationally.

"And have you told Mauro how you feel?"

"Of course!"

"Now *that* surprises me."

"But why wouldn't I tell him? He's my beau ideal, the great love of my life. Also, you can't keep things from him. He guesses."

"And what did he say?"

"He said he felt honored. And he said he loved me too, in his way . . ." Tears brimmed Nathan's eyes.

After a week? I didn't ask.

"And then he said that even though he couldn't reciprocate my feelings on a physical level," Nathan continued, "he hoped I'd stay his friend. As if I could ever be anything but his friend!"

"Celia did say he was invincibly straight."

"Oh, I'm not convinced of that! He's Italian, after all. He's had experiences with other men. No, the only reason he won't reciprocate, he says, is loyalty to Angela."

"You mean if he were single, he might?"

"I think so. That's what torments me. I can't be sure. He has this way of talking that's both very precise and very vague. And I almost resent him for it, for dangling, ever so subtly, that carrot. I mean, if he said, you know, I'm just not remotely attracted to men, it would be easier. But he won't say that. He's too rigorously honest. And so we go on, talking and talking, and what makes it all worse — or better, depending on how you look at it — is that he's absolutely immodest with me. For instance, after we play soccer, we go downstairs — we share a bathroom, you know — and he strips naked in front of me. Completely. Then he showers with the door open."

"How interesting."

"I've been tempted — but no, it's too shameful. Or shameless."

"I've heard your locker room story."

"Of course."

Ahead of us, now, Mauro's Alfa turned left. Down an unpaved road we followed him, past abandoned brick farmhouses and fruit orchards, before finally parking at the entrance to a dirt path, where he and Celia climbed out of the car.

"It's just down this way," she said, summoning us on.

Mauro bent down and picked a few clover-shaped green leaves that were growing close to the ground. "Taste," he said, handing one to each of us. "Can you say what the flavor is?"

I closed my eyes and chewed. What *was* that flavor? So familiar; yet the texture was wrong.

"I give up," I said finally.

Then Nathan said, "It's walnut. How extraordinary!"

"Bravo, Nathan! You win the prize. This is walnut grass. *Erba noce.*"

"And what's this?" Nathan pointed to an overgrown tangle of what I would have automatically taken to be weeds.

"*Mentuccia, melissa.* Herbs for roasting. And here — tonight's salad."

"Come on, guys!" The voice, remote, was Celia's, and we moved on.

At the end of the path, in a little clearing, she stood before the Olivone. It was much bigger than I'd expected, with twisted, ancient arms. Not far, across a rusted tangle of wire, some cows looked at us.

"Two thousand years old," Celia said. "Can you imagine? That means that this tree's been being cultivated since before Caesar. Since before Caesar, Lizzie!"

I simply stared. Clots of trodden olives smeared the ground under our feet. To the left, a severed branch lay in the brambles, itself the size of an ordinary olive tree.

"Three families own it," Celia went on, "and divvy up the proceeds from the oil. That branch came off a decade ago, in a thunderstorm. That same year when we were all living in New York, and you had the slumber party at your mother's house. Remember?"

"I'd prefer not to."

"Also, the bark is supposed to have medicinal properties." She picked off a piece, almost as if it were a scab. "You're supposed to chew it. Only I can't remember what it cures."

"Toothache?"

"That's *Howards End.* And look! Where the lightning struck the branch, there's a face. Two eyes, a mouth. A perfect mask, as if the branch were joined to the trunk by the face, and after the lightning, for the first time in two thousand years, that face could see! Isn't that amazing, Nathan?"

But Nathan, who was standing at a distance from the tree, looking rather pale, didn't answer.

Clouds moved in overhead. It started to drizzle.

"We should probably go," Nathan said, while Mauro gathered up the last of the *mentuccia.*

"All right," Celia answered, clearly regretful to be parted from her Olivone.

How well I remember, now, that scene! Celia enraptured by the tree, the cow across the fence, Nathan trembling to leave.

And Mauro picking salad. And me, of course, watching.

Not implicated.

The rain thickened, and we piled back into the cars.

We waited out the storm at a little restaurant the owner of which was a friend of Celia's. She fed us beet gnocchi in pumpkin sauce, accompanied by a local red wine called a Morellino. The oil on the salad, needless to say, came from the Olivone.

After the rain eased, we went home, where Celia opened a bottle of Spumante. "I want to celebrate," she said, not specifying what — her anniversary, perhaps? — while Mauro declared happily that for supper he was going to prepare a *pappardelle sul'lepre,* noodles with hare sauce, a declaration that led, in turn, to all sorts of jokes along the lines of "Waiter, there's a hare in my sauce!" The boys cut up, and cut up the herbs Mauro had gathered at the Olivone, and Celia and I got drunk and prepared the *pappardelle.* The expertise — not to mention the celerity — with which she transformed a crater of flour filled with eggs into tidy, hand-cut ribbons of pasta, I must admit, made me envious as well as doubtful of her earlier assertion that she possessed no culinary talent. Obedience — wasn't that the secret of great cookery? And hadn't she herself told me that — it seemed now a decade ago?

Thus the afternoon melted into evening. We cooked, and Celia opened a second bottle of Spumante, and as we drank it, Mauro told more bad jokes and bossed us around. As I was quickly learning, in the kitchen, his element, he commanded. Everyone, even Celia, leapt to his call, paying to him that automatic deference that is the proven expert's due. And how fastidious he was! His hair, even when he was bending over a pot, still fell in perfect black waves. Yes, it was difficult not to be entranced by Mauro's manner, in which a coat of good breeding veneered a certain wildness, even a savagery. He was like one of those tigers Victorian ladies kept for pets: radiant in his jungle sexuality despite the perfumings and bejewelings to which he was subjected — but by who? Certainly not Celia. Angela, then? Or was his aura of elegance, even of cultivation, his *own* choice? I felt fairly certain of the latter. I also felt fairly certain that if I'd had a chance to investigate, I'd have discovered that *he* didn't pull his shirttails through the leg holes of his underpants.

In the event, Celia was just putting the dinner together — just "throwing the pasta," as the Italians say — when we heard wheels crunch the gravel outside. All at once everyone quieted.

"Expecting someone?" I asked.

"No." Celia moved uneasily toward the window.

Heavy footfalls sounded. Then the kitchen door opened, and a big interruption walked in.

"Seth!" she said.

"Hi, honey, I'm home."

He kissed her.

Mauro turned away.

"What are you doing here?" Celia asked. "Is something wrong?"

"Why does something have to be wrong? I just thought I'd surprise you. After all, it's nearly our anniversary." Leaving her aside, he turned and smiled at me. "Hello, Lizzie."

"Hi, Seth," I said, accepting his hand. "Nice to see you again."

"Likewise. And Nathan."

"Seth."

They shook manfully,

"Mauro."

Mauro's gesture was to a nod what a sliver of moon is to a moon.

"So how was your drive?"

"Traffic hell. Say, is there anything to eat? I'm starved."

"Actually, we were just getting supper ready —"

"Great. Then if you all don't mind, I'll go wash up and be back in five minutes." And he lumbered out of the kitchen, a tall man, not unattractive, in a bearded, mountainous way, though a bit too much of the Bill school for my taste.

"Well, isn't this a nice surprise," Celia said when he'd gone, and poured herself another glass of Spumante.

"A very nice surprise," I echoed.

"I suppose we should set a fifth place at the table," Nathan threw in nervously.

"Never mind." Mauro was taking off his apron. "I won't be here."

"Where are you going?"

"You know that I am eating with Angela and her mother tonight."

"But if you want to stay —"

"What do you mean, Celia? We've made just enough for four. Anyway, Seth has a big appetite."

"That doesn't matter. I don't need to eat."

"You'd better watch out or the pasta will overcook. Well, goodbye, Lizzie. Goodbye, Nathan."

"Bye, Mauro."

"*Ciao.*"

"Mauro!" Rather frantically, Celia was draining the pasta.

By the time she had finished, he had already walked out the door.

In Mauro's absence, we couldn't talk to each other. We were at a loss for language, and in battered silence, Nathan and I slunk into the dining room and took our places.

"I'm afraid it's overcooked," Celia announced a few minutes later, hauling the steaming bowl into the dining room.

"I'm sure it'll be delicious," I said.

She sat down. Seth returned. "Mm, *pappardelle,*" he said, smacking his lips and clapping his hands. "I'm starved for some good cooking. Say, where's Mauro?"

"He left."

"He's eating dinner with Angela," Nathan added.

"Oh, sure. You know I've never met Angela?" Seth took Mauro's place at the head of the table.

Celia served. We all tasted.

"Celia, this isn't like you," Seth said. "It's overcooked."

"Well, I'm sorry, Seth, but you walked in just after I'd thrown it, and —"

"I think it's delicious," I thrust in.

"Me too," Nathan echoed.

"Also, the sauce is too salty."

"Speaking of too salty," I said, "did I ever tell you about the time when everyone in my family thought that no one else had bothered to salt the lima beans and so we all salted them and then we couldn't eat them?" I laughed. "Kitchen disasters. I could write a book. You should too, Celia."

"Or a cookbook," said Nathan. "Have you thought about it?"

Celia took a sip of wine. "Actually, I've had offers."

"All of which she's turned down," Seth said. "And I've never understood why! I mean, when we started this business — what, three years ago? — it was never to run it forever. Instead our plan was to do it just long enough to pay for the renovations, which we did after six months. And still she teaches, and still she complains, Too much work, too much food —"

"I do not complain!"

"Yet every time I suggest to her that she just go and make a deal with one of those publishers, she shushes me away. And it would be perfect, really! We could have kids and live an idyllic life, me doing my translations, her inventing recipes —"

"I told you, there's no point. None of the recipes are mine."

"Does that matter?"

"It's just the old tradition. I'd be lying if I made any claim to it."

"You wouldn't be the first," Nathan said.

"Originality is a joke where cooking is concerned," Seth agreed.

He had cleaned his plate, as had Nathan. (How fast men eat!) Now Celia got up to clear, and I followed her.

"Are you all right?" I asked in the kitchen.

"I'll be all right," she said. "I just wasn't expecting him."

"I know."

"It's not bad," she amplified. "Don't think I think it's bad. Just . . . something to adjust to."

She scraped her portion of the pasta, largely uneaten, into the garbage.

"Well, at least he didn't forget your anniversary," I said for stupid comfort.

"No, he didn't do that."

"Wood, right?"

"Traditionally. The modern equivalent is silverware."

Taking Mauro's salad out of the refrigerator — that salad most of which (it seemed eons ago) he had picked near the Olivone — she carried it back to the table.

We all went to our rooms fairly soon after that miserable dinner had ended — all of us, that is, except for Seth, who announced he was going to sit a little while in the garden.

In the bathroom, I performed my ritual ablutions. To be truthful, everything about the evening — Seth's arrival, Celia's unhappiness at Seth's arrival, Mauro's rather abrupt departure — bewildered me. It was as if Seth's mere presence had thrown off some delicate balance in the *podere;* yet why was that? He didn't seem to me to be such a bad fellow. A bit arrogant, yes; still, well-meaning, enthusiastic. Nonetheless Mauro clearly despised him, while Celia, in his presence, changed completely; became awkward, inept. And why should that be? Why should this husband to whom she professed indifference, this husband she barely ever saw, still hold such power over her? I didn't know the answer, though I suspected that if Bill had walked in while we were cooking, his unexpected arrival might have reduced me, too, to a state of anxious incompetence. Love's poison, I've noticed, has a way of lingering in the body even years after love itself has withdrawn its fangs.

In bed, tired out from the expedition to the Olivone (not to mention all that Spumante), I fell asleep at once. Then I was in the middle of having a complicated dream about Bill when a loud crashing sounded, and I leapt up in bed. What I'd experienced is known technically as a myoclonic jerk, and in my dream it had taken the form of a leap off a mountain into an abyss from which the arms of waking seemed to trapeze me upward. I looked around myself, saw the crystal diodes of the alarm clock glowing. One forty-four A.M. Then the noise — more like furniture moving than a crash, my refining mind noted — sounded again.

I listened. I heard a voice, deep-throated. Like the furniture-moving noise, it came from downstairs.

"*Si, cosi. Cosi.*"

Well, I'll be damned, I thought. Maybe Nathan's managed to get him after all.

A door slammed. From the hallway voices broke out.

"Celia, stop!" (This in a whisper-scream.)

"Let go of me!"

"It's none of your business, Celia!"

"I said let go of me!"

Scrapings and thumpings. Alarmed, I switched on the light, pulled on a bathrobe, and stepped into the hall, where as expected, I found Seth in his pajamas, struggling to restrain a maniacal Celia in a Lanz nightgown patterned with little lambs. Their futile efforts to keep their voices down only made the battle seem more surreal, as if it were taking place in slow motion.

"What's going on?"

"Lizzie, will you please try to talk some sense into her? She's going nuts."

"Celia, what's the matter?"

She kicked Seth and fled. "Shit!" he said, "I give up," and returned to their bedroom. Meanwhile I followed Celia down the stairs, through the living room, and to the bottom floor, where she rapped loudly on Nathan's door.

"Get out!" she shouted. "Both of you! Get out! Seth thought it was you," she added to me, "if you can believe it. I knew better."

The door opened. Nathan, pulling on his pants, stepped into the hall.

"Just what in the hell do you think you're doing?"

"I could ask you the same question. Now get out of my house. You too, Mauro!"

"Quiet!" Nathan pulled the door shut. "Anyway, he won't hear you. He's out."

"Don't lie to me."

"No, I mean drunk."

"Then wake him! Throw water on him!"

"Celia, please!" Nathan grabbed her by the arm. "What's gotten into you?"

Kicking *him* hard, she ran into the kitchen.

"Christ!" Nathan said. "That bi——" He made a fist. "This is really the last straw, Lizzie. What, does she have to spoil the best night in my life because seventeen years ago I wouldn't fuck her —"

"Were you and Mauro —"

"So what if we were? Is there something wrong with that?"

"I'm only asking so I can figure out —"

We stepped through the kitchen door.

"I said get out!" Celia screamed, throwing a plate at Nathan.

"Stop!"

She threw another plate. "You moron! You prick!"

"Don't throw things!"

"You don't care about anything except your goddamn dick, do you? You'd sell your sister to a bunch of rapists if you thought one of them would let you suck his cock —"

"Celia —"

"You'd betray anyone, you'd sell your mother into white slavery —"

"Shut up about my mother!"

"I hate you! I despise you! Get out of my house!"

Once again she stormed away, out into the garden.

"Then at least tell me *why* you despise me," Nathan said, giving chase under the stars. (And me giving chase to Nathan.) "I mean, what's happened between Mauro and me — I'm sorry, but it's none of your business. Maybe Angela's —"

"You idiot! There is no Angela! I'm Angela!"

He stopped. "Oh, Jesus . . ."

"*I'm* Angela. *Me. I'm* the girlfriend." She was crying now. "Lizzie, didn't you see it?"

"No," I said.

"Are you blind? Are you both blind? I love him more than —"

"Oh shit," Nathan said. "But I didn't know! He just said, he kept repeating, 'She's gone back to him,' and so I assumed —"

"It's too late."

"Why didn't you tell me?"

"Celia!" Seth's voice this time.

"I can't face him," she said, then started away, out into the fields. In the distance, I could hear the echo-music of cowbells.

"Celia!"

"Don't," I said, and held out my arm to block Nathan.

"But —"

"Let her go."

"What on earth is going on?" Seth asked, bursting into the garden.

"She needs time alone. She's upset."

"Why?"

"Can't you guess?"

Seth stepped back, taking it for granted in his egotism (and perhaps even gratified) that he himself had caused the rupture. Then he went into the house.

"As if it isn't enough —" Nathan said.

"Oh, it's not enough," I said. "For her it's never been enough." And returning to the kitchen, I started sweeping up the broken plates.

All that night I swept. First the kitchen floor, then the living room. Then I cleaned out the refrigerator. Then I wiped off all the kitchen counters, my eyes perpetually watching for some movement of the doorknob that never occurred. And though I can't pretend my suspicions about what had happened to Celia forged themselves over the course of that single long night, nor even over the course of the long days that followed — days during which Nathan and I guarded the fort and cooked and made coffee while Mauro and Seth, thrown into uneasy allegiance by disaster, scoured the countryside for their disappeared lover and bride — nonetheless it was that night that the questions started to accrete. Why *had* Celia, from the very beginning, not only not discouraged Nathan's friendship with Mauro, but actively thrown them at each other? Put Nathan in the room next to Mauro's, when she could have put him in my room? Urged them to drive to that *enoteca* in Siena, and smiled blithely as they played soccer together, and at that last dinner allowed Seth, literally, to eclipse Mauro's place so that when Nathan prepared for him that bower wherein the waters of comfort coax carnality into bud, his resistance level was low? Too low.

We talked about it. Nathan suggested that perhaps Celia was a masochist, attending with loving concentration to the decoration of that coffin in which her own short-lived happiness would be interred. As for me, I remembered something I'd forgotten, a last snippet of one of our conversations. (Or did Celia tell me this in a dream, waving a flashlight onto the past, onto the one bit of broken china I hadn't swept away?) As you recall I'd suggested that Nathan's treatment of her over the years might have resulted from her wearing the psychological equivalent of a kick-me sign. What I'd forgotten was this response: "Well, what of it, Lizzie? I mean, isn't that the proof of love, when in spite of the kick-me sign, someone doesn't kick you?"

About eight o'clock on the morning of our departure, grimy from days of panic, Nathan and I walked into Montesepolcro to get some coffee. Mauro had driven off already on his morning sweep of the countryside, while Seth, having taken three Valium, was still in bed.

We only stopped when just outside the village wall a cow walked into the road and blocked our path.

Nathan moved to the right. The cow followed.

He moved to the left. The cow followed.

"What?"

The cow looked at him.

Suddenly a cluster of flies maddened the sky.

"Not . . . possible," Nathan said, driving his hands through his hair. And the cow moved her hard, implacable jaw.

Saturn Street

In Los Angeles, in the early 1990s, I spent a couple of months delivering lunches to homebound people with AIDS under the auspices of a group of men and women who called themselves the Angels. I did this neither to make myself look virtuous, nor to alleviate some deep-seated guilt: the usual motives for volunteerism. Instead I viewed the matter pragmatically. I had a car, and nowhere to go in the mornings. So I brought food.

The Angels operated out of a Methodist rectory on Formosa Avenue. A mood of unrelenting cheerfulness always prevailed in that place. In the kitchen women whose sons had died or were dying stirred sauces and baked pies under the supervision of fussy West Hollywood chefs, while near the door three ex-actors — two Keiths and a Wayne — handed out client manifests and route maps to the drivers. Having been assigned a route, I'd pack the meals I was to deliver that morning in brown paper bags, like school lunches, then haul them out to the car. Some of the clients got soft meals, some liquid meals. For those who needed it, food was supplemented by a canned drink called Sustical, a sort of calorie-packed milk shake (the client's preferred flavor, strawberry or chocolate, was always specified on the manifest); or by a clear emulsion, mostly rice syrup solids, that promised quick rehydration after diarrhea. As for the regular lunches, they were by design very fattening, since the best way to keep the body from consuming itself is to lard it with rich foods. At a moment in our history notorious for its devotion to dishes described as "light," "low-fat" or "nonfat," the Angels drenched their vegetables in butter, dolloped slices of pecan pie with whipped cream, sopped chicken thighs in yolky batters.

The routes I followed varied. Some days I'd travel east, to Normandie Avenue and Western Avenue, where most of the clients were drug users living in squalid residential hotels. Or I'd drive up into the Hollywood Hills to bring lunches to movie producers and soap opera actors. Or I'd deliver along that flat net of geometric streets that stretches southwest from Santa Monica toward Olympic Boulevard, streets in which one block of cheap apartments blurs randomly into another. (Only a few stand out in memory: the Killarney, painted a lurid shade of Irish green; the Mikado, with its dilapidated pagoda turrets, its windows *à la japonaise.*)

Most of my clients didn't talk to me. They were embarrassed faces, mouths muttering "thank you" even as the deadbolt turned. But a few invited me in. A woman called Wilma Rodriguez always had a glass of iced papaya tea waiting when I arrived. She lived in one room in a building called the Caribou Arms on San Marino Street. "I don't know how I got it," she told me once. "Maybe it was from shooting heroin. Or maybe it was my gay ex-husband. Or maybe it was the blood transfusions after the car accident." She had that kind of gallant gallows humor — what I can only call AIDS humor — that the healthy find so astounding. A few weeks after I met her, Wilma came down with a brain fever and died in a matter of hours.

No doubt the strangest of my clients was a young man called Robert Franklin. He lived on Beverly Glen Boulevard, that tortured helix of a road that twists upward from Pico in Rancho Park, crosses Mulholland Drive, then winds down into the oppressive flatness of Sherman Oaks. A phrase from a book I had just read about Italy during the Second World War — "cloud-cuckoo land" — sticks in my mind whenever I remember the series of staggered, rickety wooden staircases I had to climb to get to Robert's little house, which sat perched on stilts at the top of a weed-choked incline, and on the splintery porch of which he always waited for me, naked except for orange tennis shoes and an IV that he dragged around like some ill-behaved terrier.

"You're late," he snapped the first time I delivered to him. "You were supposed to be here an hour ago."

"I got held up. Also, you were at the end of my route."

"Excuses, excuses." Robert peered suspiciously into the bag I had just handed him. "And what have we here, pray tell?"

"Shepherd's pie —"

"Shepherd's pie! Didn't they tell you I absolutely loathe shepherd's pie?"

"It doesn't say on the manifest —"

"Plus it's almost two. I told you people distinctly, my doctor says I'm supposed to eat lunch before one. Otherwise the medicine won't absorb."

"I'll make a note —"

"Whatever happened to service? The tightest ship in the shipping business, my ass." (He fiddled with his IV.)

"Well, goodbye," I said.

"If this goes on, I tell you, I'm switching back to the good old P.O."

"Is there anything else you need?"

"Only to have my packages delivered on time. I mean," he shouted as I descended the staircase, "this is supposed to be America. Is it too much to ask to have your packages delivered on time?"

At the time I hadn't been living in Los Angeles very long. By breeding and disposition, I'm a New Yorker; indeed, I had come to California only for the most banal and clichéd of reasons: I had fallen for an actor and, needing an excuse to follow him west, taken on a commission to do a television screenplay about growing up in the sixties, a sort of spin-off from an essay I'd written a decade earlier. But the actor dumped me a few days after I arrived, at which point I developed a case of writer's block so severe that until I started delivering for the Angels, I was spending most of my days talking dirty on phone sex lines, or cruising the parking lot next to the Circus of Books, or wandering through the Glendale Galleria, occasionally buying something overpriced and useless: a bottle of Swiss skin moisturizer, or a foot massager, or a "Sony Dinner Classics" CD complete with recipes. I drove a rented car and lived in a West Hollywood hotel room, both paid for by the development company that had commissioned the screenplay. My employers never called me to ask how my work was going; indeed, never called me, period. It was my impression that they had writers cubbyholed all over town, far too many to keep track of, and none lower priority than myself. As for the car and the hotel room, these represented for the company the most trivial of tax deductions, the equivalent of what writing off thirty-seven cents' worth of stamps, or the cost of a Bic pen, would have been for me.

Sometimes I thought of phoning Dr. Delia. Dr. Delia was a radio psychotherapist whose live call-in program (1-800-DR-DELIA) aired every weekday from eleven to one, exactly the hours I spent in my car delivering for the Angels. Dr. Delia had a demented cackle and a savage sense of rectitude. She was deaf to pleas for pity, felt no qualms in telling her callers (mostly young women) just how stupid or selfish or irresponsible they'd been in getting pregnant, or marrying drunks, or going to bed with strangers. Indeed, so insistent a companion was Dr. Delia on my rounds that now it is her voice, as crisp as newly ironed sheets, that narrates my memory of these events, reading the words back to me even as I look them over on the computer screen.

I used to make a game of planning what I'd say if I ever called Dr. Delia myself. For instance: Dr. Delia, I'm a thirty-five-year-old writer who can't write. The person I loved most killed himself a few months back. Now I watch porn videos and call phone sex lines obsessively.

All right. What's your question?

How do I get back to who I was, or who I used to think I was? That boy — productive, energetic, unburdened?

But in this fantasy, just as Dr. Delia is about to answer me, the same thing happens that happened whenever I drove under a bridge, or into a garage, or by a police station: her voice disappears into leaps and squeals of static.

After I dropped off my last meal, I made it my habit to drive over to the Circus of Books on Santa Monica Boulevard and return the videos I had rented the night before. I always rented my videos at the Circus of Books, not only because the store had such a big selection, but because as I lingered behind the frosted Plexiglas door that said "Over Eighteen Only," picking among the films like an Italian housewife choosing vegetables for her minestrone, invariably I would encounter three or four other men doing the same thing, and some of them would be dressed in cutoff sweatpants with no underwear. I had a thing about cutoff sweatpants with no underwear.

Today I chose *Barracks Detention,* which was new, as well as *Pump It Up,* which I remembered having watched with Julian in the late eighties. It's funny the things that become enmeshed in that web of tenderness that underlies every marriage, even the worst one: not just flowers and fields and half-moons of heart-stopping luminosity, but also squeezing the pimples on a loved one's back, or sitting on the toilet while he brushes his teeth, or watching pornography together: something Julian and I did, like everything else we did, compulsively. A little less than nine months had passed since his suicide. Now I found that rewatching the porn videos we'd looked at side by side in our New York bed eased the ache of his swollen and enflamed nonpresence. The porn videos were psychic Shiatsu, fingers rubbing the sorest kink I'd ever known. They made me want to scream, but somehow I knew that only by suffering them might I unknot the ligaments of grief.

Two was always the formula. The future and the past. Adventure and nostalgia. Memory and desire. Having made my selections, I'd then head back to the hotel, check my voice-mail messages (there were usually none), switch the air conditioner on high, and take the first of the videos — this time

Barracks Detention — out of the box. All as I undressed: I was a master at pushing buttons with my toes while switching on lamps with my fingers, pulling off socks with one hand while inserting cassettes with the other. "Always doing two things at once," Julian used to say. He called it the "Rosemary Woods Dance," after Nixon's secretary, who'd revealed the latent skills of a contortionist upon being asked to explain "accidentally" erasing the tapes; which, over the course of years, got abbreviated to "doing a Rosemary." Perhaps marital conversation always evolves into such shorthand.

In any event, having put on *Barracks Detention,* I propped myself up in the bed. With my right hand I dialed the phone sex number. With my left I fast-forwarded through the assurances that all the models were over eighteen ("proof of age on file"), the admonishments not to try this at home, the credit sequence.

The world of the porn videos intrigued me. About their making I knew very little, though I did have a German friend in New York who told me that sometimes he made extra cash working as a "stunt dick." A stunt dick, as he explained it, was a kind of sexual understudy who waited in the wings only to be brought in if one of the models in the video couldn't get it up, or couldn't ejaculate, or proved to have a smaller penis than anticipated; in such circumstances, close-ups of the stunt dick's dick were spliced into the footage in the hope that the viewer wouldn't notice the substitution. "And it happens more than you think," my German friend added. "Next time you watch, keep an eye on the editing."

I took my finger off the fast-forward button. On the screen two lanky young men, one with bad teeth, lay on cots. They were wearing khaki-colored boxer shorts and dog tags, conversing about . . . something; though I'd switched off the volume, I knew from experience that the dialogue was probably running something along these lines:

Luke: Scott! How's it hanging, dude?
Scott: Not bad, Luke. Yourself?
Luke: Can't complain. Found some dirty pictures in the Sarge's desk. Have a look?
Scott: Sounds like a winner.
(*Pause.*)
Luke: Gee, that thing's getting pretty hard. Want me to suck it?
Scott: Sounds like a winner.
(*Pause.*)
Luke: Hey, Scott, ever fucked another guy?
Scott: No.
Luke: Bet my asshole'll feel better than your girlfriend's cunt.
Scott: Sounds like a winner.

And so on. The phone sex line picked up, interrupting this little reverie. Following the prompts, I punched in my access code. "Are you ready?" said that breathy recorded voice on the other end with which I had become, over the weeks, at least as familiar as I was with Dr. Delia's. "Do you know what you want? Do it . . . now." (Music.) "Press one if you want to talk to one other guy at a time; press two for the group; press three for the audio bulletin board —"

I pressed one.

"And remember, if you finish with one conversation, just press the pound sign — that's the button under the number nine — and you'll be automatically reconnected with somebody else. Oh, and of course, zero always returns you to the main menu. Your connection is being made." Click.

"Hello?"

"Hey, who's this?"

"Jerry, who's this?"

"Steve. Where're you calling from, bud?"

"West Hollywood."

"Shit, I'm in Long Beach. Good luck, man." Click.

Again, that breathy voice. (Who did it belong to?)

"Please hold on just a second while your connection is being made." A running loop of music.

I turned my attention back to the video, in the utopia of which the boxer shorts had come off; the sucking had commenced.

I didn't have a hard-on. The truth was, I didn't feel horny at all. "Failure is forming habits"— wasn't it Pater who said that? And certainly anyone who might have seen me at that moment, naked on a hotel bed with a phone cradled against my neck, not really watching the video I had rented, my pathetic posture not even dignified by an erection, for God's sake — well, that person would have deemed me the most dismal of failures. Dr. Delia would have deemed me the most dismal of failures, and in no uncertain terms.

In the world of the phone line, of course, none of this signified. In that pocket of consciousness defined only by sound, the blind led the blind. Subjects became objects. The fat fifty-year-old man became the twenty-year-old football hero he'd adored when he was twenty. "How long have you been here?" people sometimes asked, presupposing that there *was* a "here," that so many voices defined a physical space, a place. But they did. All those voices defined it, tendriling the complex weave of fiber-optic cables like some voracious species of vine.

A beep sounded. "Your connection is being made," the breathy voice said.

"Hello?"

"Hi, what's your name? I'm Doug."

"Hey, Doug, I'm Jerry. How you doing, buddy?"

"Great, dude. You?"

"Great, pal. Real horny."

"Yeah? So listen, sport, you looking to connect or just get off on the phone?"

"I don't know, guy, maybe connect." (Only connect.)

"Sounds hot, champ. What do you get into?"

"Pretty versatile. Like jacking off a lot. More a bottom than a top."

"Cool. What's your dick like?"

"Seven and a half long, five around."

"Let me hear it."

"Hear it?"

"Slap it against the phone."

Now this was something new.

"Okay," I said, then, putting the receiver under the covers, did what Doug had requested of me.

After a few slaps I lifted the receiver to my ear again. "Hello?" I said.

"Sounds big," Doug said. "Thick."

"Can you really tell?"

"Sure you can. A small dick makes a small noise. Now listen to mine."

I listened. In the distance I could hear the faintest tapping, a kind of castanet clack.

"Like it?" Doug asked after a few seconds.

What was there to say? "Yeah, I like it."

Click.

"Please hold on just a second while your connection is being made —"

I hung up.

When I arrived at the rectory the next morning, the second of the Keiths smiled at me in a way that I knew meant he had a favor to ask. "We're changing your route," he said. "Hope you don't mind. Gin's back from vacation, and she always does Beverly Glen."

"No problem." It was my policy not to make problems. "Just warn her about Robert Franklin and the shepherd's pie."

"Is he complaining again? It's better to ignore him. Listen, if it's okay, we wondered if we might give you Olympic South. That's out toward the airport."

"Sounds like a winner."

We went over the manifest, after which I packed up my lunches and headed out. The route in question took me down La Cienega, past Olympic, and toward Venice Boulevard. Here some of the cross streets had extraordinary names: Cadillac Avenue, Airdrome Street, Saturn Street. And it was on Saturn Street, number 6517 to be precise, that my last delivery lived. Phil Featherstone. Apartment 25. No fish. "If not home, leave lunch with #24."

Dr. Delia was taking a call from Trish in West Covina. "So here's my problem, Doctor," Trish was saying. "The other day I caught my husband, Todd, like, flirting with my best girlfriend."

"How old are you?"

"Twenty."

"And how old is Todd?"

"He's twenty-two."

"Uh-huh. Any kids?"

"Yes, two. Kirsty's three and Tiffany's six months."

"And how long did you and Todd date before you got married?"

"I don't see what that has to do with —"

"Don't talk back to me. How long did you and Todd date before you got married?"

"Well, we dated about three weeks, then we lived together about six weeks, then —"

"Wait a second. Am I hearing this right? You're twenty years old, and you married a guy you only knew nine weeks? Don't you think that's kind of *stupid*?"

On the other end of the line, an almost palpably stunned silence.

"Well, no. We loved each other —"

"You *loved* each other. Oh, isn't that sweet —"

A car honked, urging me through the stop sign. Number 6517 Saturn Street approached, a pleasant bottle-green building called The Rings. For a moment I considered not stopping, driving around the block to find out what further humiliations Dr. Delia would inflict upon Trish, but then I decided that driving around the block to hear Dr. Delia was too much like driving around the parking lot next to the Circus of Books, looking for sex — in addition to which "Phil Featherstone" was probably getting hungry. It was past one-thirty. So I pulled up to the curb and switched off the radio as well as the ignition.

At the door to the building I rang the bell for number 25. "Yes?" a voice answered after a few seconds.

"Angels."

An electrocuting buzz sounded, then the mechanical clank

of the door unlocking itself. Not surprisingly, the apartments were ranged in rings (what else?) around a kidney-shaped swimming pool in which some desultory children floated bath toys. Number 25 was on the upper story. The door had been left open. For the sake of politeness I knocked anyway.

"Come in!"

I stepped inside. The apartment looked to me like what I imagined the hotel rooms of sequestered jurors must look like: drab furniture, dirty beige carpeting, walls stuccoed as if they'd been slathered with cake frosting. And yet accretions of the personal were making their claim: a poster depicting the crew of the *Enterprise* from *Star Trek,* framed snapshots of babies, some barbells in a corner.

A handsome man stepped out from the kitchenette. In his late thirties, I guessed, with graying brown hair, green eyes, and a thick beard, closely cropped, in which red, gray, and brown combined to create almost pointillist scintillations.

"Hey, I'm Phil," he said, and offered me his hand.

"I'm Jerry Roth," I said. We shook. I gave him two bags. "I've got an extra today if you can use it. Someone earlier on the route wasn't home, and we have a policy against leaving food on people's doorsteps."

"Great," Phil said. "Thanks." Taking the bags from me, he carried them to his refrigerator. "Listen, would you like something to drink? I don't know if you're in a hurry —"

"Actually I'm not. It's the end of my route."

"Terrific. I've got Pepsi, Dr. Pepper, orange juice. No beer. The doctors nixed that."

"Water would be fine."

"One water coming up." He took some glasses down from a cabinet. "Have a seat, by the way."

The brown vinyl of the sofa creaked as I eased into it.

"This is a nice apartment," I said. "Sunny."

"Thanks. You know, I've only been with the program a week now. And every day a different guy comes. Is that normal?"

Suddenly he was leaning over me, handing me water. He had on a blue polo shirt and cutoff sweatpants, the polo shirt open at the throat, exposing a triangular patch of broad-beamed, hairy chest.

"This route's a tough one to assign," I said. "The problem is, most of the volunteers live in West Hollywood or the Valley. They want to stay close to home. But my philosophy is, whatever no one else wants, give me. At the very least, it's a great way to learn the city."

"Oh, it's not a problem," Phil said, sitting down in a floral armchair. "In fact, it's something to look forward to. Every morning I think, Who's it going to be this time? And always a surprise."

"I hope not a disappointment, in my case."

"No," Phil said, laughing a little. "Not a disappointment."

A silence now descended, one that would have been awkward, had Phil's grin not assured me, in its radiant ease, that silence was okay. I gulped my water, chewed ice.

"I don't know this neighborhood very well," I said, to fill the air.

"Not much to know. Basically it's pretty bland. I just like Saturn Street because of the name."

"The name?"

"Yeah. It's like something from an old science fiction movie. Also, it was one of the first street names I noticed when I moved to L.A. I didn't start here right away, though. I've lived all over. Venice. Silver Lake. Out in the desert a couple of years. Then one day I'm looking to find a new place, and I see this ad in the paper for an apartment on Saturn Street. And I think, Who knows? Maybe it's a sign. So I took it. That was a few months ago, just before I got sick."

"I see."

He leaned closer. "Listen," he said, "I wondered if I could ask you something. Because this AIDS thing — it's all kind of new for me. Before, I was always healthy as an ox. Then one day about six months ago I wake up with this cough and twelve hours later" — he snapped his fingers — "boom, I'm in the hospital. And what I'm wondering is, what are you supposed to think when a thing like that happens? How do you negotiate it? What do you do?"

I choked. I felt like Miss America being asked to solve world hunger.

"Well, here in L.A. there are a lot of services available. For instance, if you want, AIDS Project L.A. will find you a buddy —"

"Oh, I know that. I've got a buddy. He comes Tuesdays and Thursdays."

"Okay, let's see. Masseurs for Life gives free massages. Then there's an organization of dentists that does teeth cleaning. Oh, have you got a pet?"

"No."

"Because if you did, PAWS would walk it, or take care of it if you had to go into the hospital. I'm trying to think what else. Would you like to write a living will? There's a group of lawyers that does them up free. I can get the number if you're —"

Phil shook his head. "To be honest, Jerry, I'm not looking for organizations. I'm looking for a philosophy. Which I guess really isn't something someone else can give you, though with you people who maybe know the territory better than I do, I always like to inquire." He leaned back in his chair. "It's just that in my case it all happened so suddenly. Now, if I'd gotten tested — I mean, that's the one advantage. You have time to prepare. But back then, I figured, why get tested when all it means is that you have to live with bad news? It was the devil you know versus the devil you don't know, only I chose the one you don't know. And of course no one ever could give me a decent reason to get tested. Oh sure, the papers were saying for a while that early AZT postponed the symptoms, but I never believed it, and now it turns out to be a crock. So I don't regret it. I just . . ." He faltered. "I suppose I just assumed, in my heart of hearts, that I was negative. I felt sure of it. So the pneumonia, when it came, came as a shock."

He looked away, not toward the window but toward the television, the *Star Trek* poster.

"And how are you feeling now?"

"Worse than I look."

"You look good."

"That won't last long, I'm told."

Certain truths you don't argue with. You just accept them.

For lack of anything better, I fell back on Angels P.R.-speak. "Well, a nutritious meal may help more than you realize," I said. "Today there's chicken-fried steak with applesauce, Cobb salad, chocolate cheesecake . . ."

Phil laughed again. "Don't worry," he said. "I'll eat anything but fish." He played with his beard. "And if you don't mind my asking, what else do you do, Mr. Jerry Roth, besides deliver meals to pathetic guys like me?"

"Oh, I guess I'm a writer."

"You guess?"

"I'm not getting much done these days. I used to write . . . I don't know how to describe it. Personal nonfiction? But now I'm working, or I should be working, on a screenplay. I live in New York most of the time, by the way. I'm only here a couple of months." Almost apologetically, I smiled. "How about you?"

"Oh, me, I've done a bunch of stuff. The last couple of years I had my own business. Carpentry. I advertised in the gay papers. Now that's gone to the dogs." He reached over his shoulder to scratch his neck. "So these days I just sit around here waiting for cute guys like you to bring me lunch, Jerry." And he grinned again: a grin so winning, so bright in its promises, I had to laugh, to turn away. A pleasant rush, almost erotic, blew through me; a sort of hot wind of gratification. Meanwhile Phil stretched his arms. For an instant his shirt rode up. I could see a stripe of hairy stomach, the navel shadowed. Why, even now a fusion of sensations seizes me as I remember the rising of his shirt, sensations so garbled that separating them out would be like trying to pull the primary colors from a swatch of gray: all those bright, basic emotions — eros and pity, affection and dread — muddying in the onrushing blur of a lived moment.

I got up. I said I had to go. "The typewriter beckons," I joked.

"You still use a typewriter?"

"No, no. I use a computer. Just a figure of speech." I held out my hand. "Well, it's been nice meeting you, Phil."

"It's been nice meeting you, Jerry," Phil said. And putting his hand against the small of my back, he walked me to the door.

"Listen, will you be driving this route again?"

"I can request it. I'm sure they won't mind. Like I said, this one can be tough to assign. Who knows? Maybe I can make your route my route — on a permanent basis. Although that would mean losing the element of surprise."

"Oh, I wouldn't mind losing *that,*" Phil said, and from his tone of voice I sensed that he meant it: that mysteriously, I had started mattering to him.

We shook hands. I left. I didn't look back. Instead I listened for the door to close, which it didn't. And how remarkable: even now I feel it, that sensation of burning, like a patch of fever, where Phil had rested his palm on the small of my back. I feel it in the very same spot.

A confession now, before I continue: like Phil, I had never been tested. Indeed, my refusal to be tested had been the main reason my actor boyfriend had dumped me, or, to put it as he put it, "elected to terminate our relationship at an early stage." In retrospect, I don't blame Trent. After all, he had tested negative sixteen times. In me he was hoping to find a companion with whom he might migrate to the arcadia of the saved, a place I think he envisioned as being akin to one of those ritzy condominium complexes in North Hollywood, with electric fences and security guards and ID badges. So far as I could tell Trent negotiated his life according to two principles: a naive faith in documentation, and a terror of illness so stunning he would sometimes drive ten blocks out of his way not to pass a hospital. In other words, he couldn't live *not* knowing he was negative. Whereas I couldn't live knowing I was positive. Death was fear for me too, and in this regard, despite our skewed responses, Trent and I had something in common. As Phil had said, it was the devil you knew versus the devil you didn't know, only in our fixation on choosing between devils, Trent and I forgot one thing: angels also walk among us.

Julian had always linked my refusal to be tested with what he called my "time problem." According to Julian, I lived too much in the future. I was forever second-guessing, speaking before I thought, looking forward so hard to the next event that I missed the lived moment even as it was happening. He liked to tease me about this. "Stop," he'd say. "Don't look. Who's standing behind you?"

"A woman?"

"What color coat is she wearing?"

"Red?"

"Did you see that, or did you just guess?"

Usually I just guessed. I didn't absorb details well. After a dinner party, I couldn't remember the furniture. Whereas Julian took in every flounce, every bit of detailing. He could recite back color schemes as if he were *Architectural Digest.* He noticed the world he lived in, perhaps too much. His mind was an attic stored with heirlooms, not one of which he could bear to toss away. The accumulated wreckage left less and less room for identity, and that threw him into a panic.

Me, I was selectively blind. I took in only the things that bore on what was coming next. I resisted like hell that examined life into which Julian tried to lead me — Julian, whose own life was, if this is possible, overexamined — because to examine my life would have been to examine the fearful inexorability of death. A truth that Julian, in his vicious final flameout, brought home harder than I ever imagined possible.

The HIV test aggravated the problem. The trouble for me was the accordionlike nature of time perception. Happiness scrunched a month into a second. Dread stretched a week into a light year. I couldn't bear the prospect of waiting for test results any more than I could bear the prospect of waiting for disease. Better the unknown devil, I figured, the unexamined life.

Of course, Dr. Delia would have put a different spin on things. Dr. Delia would have said that I was resisting getting tested because underneath it all I didn't want the thing with Trent to work out. To which theory I can only respond: well, maybe. It's certainly possible that I harbored some masochistic yen to short-circuit my own erotic happiness, or deny the finality of Julian's departure. And yet I can't ignore the fact that it wasn't merely the gesture of getting tested that Trent wanted me to make; if I'd tested positive, he'd have dumped me too.

Actually, it was Dr. Delia who had directed me to the Angels in the first place. One afternoon, a few weeks after I'd arrived in L.A., I was driving around aimlessly, listening to her program, when with great whoops of self-congratulation she announced that she had recently spent a morning delivering meals. She went on to explain who the Angels were, how they worked, what a marvelous experience it had been to drive for them and meet their clients, who showed such stoicism in the face of adversity. "It makes me really wonder about you people," she told her listeners. "You call me up, you whine like a bunch of babies, when all the time you're blessed with the gift of life. Then I meet these folks who *really* have something on their plates, and do they gripe? Do they moan? Not one bit. Think about that the next time you feel like calling."

Well, I don't know what it was about that little sermon, but the next morning I drove straight to Angels headquarters. Wayne and the Keiths were delighted if somewhat surprised by my breathless entrance, my bumbling, "Hello, I want to deliver." Within minutes I was bagging lunches, and within minutes after that winding my way up Beverly Glen Boulevard, to Robert Franklin's house. Would Dr. Delia have been proud? Would Julian have been proud? I couldn't say.

But to get back to Phil: the next morning, I asked the second of the Keiths whether I might take on the Olympic South route on a semipermanent basis. He acceded willingly, glad to palm off a tough neighborhood. Then I went to bag. Something of a ruckus had started up in the kitchen. It seemed that a young actress, the star of a new sitcom about college roommates, had come to deliver that morning, bringing along an *Entertainment Tonight* reporter as if he were an afterthought. "I feel so good about what I'm doing!" this actress was now explaining to the reporter. "It makes me feel just great to help these people out." After which a camera crew filmed her smiling as she sorted meals; smiling as she bagged; smiling as she chatted with Sunny Duvall, the Angels' unofficial leader. (Some people called her the "archangel.")

All of this I tried to ignore. To me it was obvious that what motivated this young creature's giggliness wasn't the joy of doing good works so much as the knowledge that only through continuous exposure to the cameras could she make her fledgling fame stick. Not surprising: in Hollywood acts of generosity usually have profit margins. And yet if any of the other Angels felt the way I did, they didn't show it. Indeed, not only didn't they look disgusted when the camera crew jostled them out of the kitchen, or asked them to clear the table where the actress was bagging, they went along with these demands good-naturedly. The humming atmosphere of altruism became yet another soundstage. Mostly out-of-work actors themselves, the Angels gave wide berth to the orgy of mutual back-scratching that the actress's agent had no doubt days ago proposed to Sunny, pointing out how much a spot on *Entertainment Tonight* would benefit them too. Even the clients, I later learned, got in on the act, vying for the opportunity to be part of the "representative" routes Sunny worked out every time a celebrity came to deliver.

Needless to say, it was the rare celebrity who delivered when the cameras weren't rolling.

I was loading my lunches into the boxes I used to carry them out to the car when a little bell rang, indicating that the prayer circle was about to start. Usually I tried to be out of headquarters by the time the prayer circle started; today, however, the brouhaha surrounding the actress had slowed me down.

Conversation quieted. Very efficiently all the Angels except me left off what they were doing and stepped to the center of the rectory. They joined hands. Next Sunny Duvall spoke an innocuous benediction: "Dear God, who is love, bless this food," etc. The actress stood on one side of her, the *Entertainment Tonight* reporter on the other. Cameras swerved in to get a close-up of the girl's face.

"Does anyone have anything to share?" Sunny asked.

"I'd like to request a moment of silence for Tommy on Normandie near Sixth, who passed away yesterday," a woman with blue hair said.

"Let us have a moment of silence for Tommy," Sunny intoned.

Silence.

"Anything else?"

"I'd like to offer a round of applause for Leah, who's recently joined our kitchen staff," the second of the Keiths said.

"Applause for Leah!" Sunny said.

Applause.

"Anything else?"

"I just want to say how great you guys are!" This was the actress.

"Applause for us!"

More applause. The prayer circle broke up. For about five minutes everybody kissed everybody else indiscriminately. Then we all went back to bagging.

Just as I was getting ready to leave, Sunny sauntered over to me. We hadn't been formally introduced. Sunny was also an actress. A decade earlier she'd made a fortune doing a series of commercials in which she played, of all things, Mother Nature; indeed, she had become so closely identified with that role that her career was largely ruined as a consequence. Now she lived off residuals, as well as occasional appearances in shopping malls.

"Hello, Jerry, I'm Sunny," she said to me now, offering her hand. "I just wanted to say thanks for all the help you've given us. Wayne tells me you've delivered every day for a month now. That's fantastic."

"It's been a pleasure," I said.

"The one thing I've noticed, though, is that you haven't joined our prayer circle. Why is that? Do you have a problem with prayer?"

I looked up. She was smiling. Her Mother Nature teeth gleamed, almost blinding.

"It's just not my thing," I said, adding by way of explanation, "I'm from New York."

As if she were being held at gunpoint, Sunny put her hands

in the air. "Oh, don't think I'm trying to pressure you! I'm not. I just want to suggest you give it a try. Who knows? It might make you feel good. Well, thanks again." And, kissing my forehead, she wandered off into the crowd.

I got in my car and drove south, toward Olympic. Since I knew the territory now, my deliveries went more quickly than they had the day before. By one I was cruising down Saturn Street, listening as Dr. Delia chatted with Gwyn in Calabasas.

"Hi, Doctor," Gwyn said. "My problem is this. I'm a forty-nine-year-old divorcée and I've fallen in love with a younger guy."

"How young is younger?"

"Twenty-three."

"Wow, that's younger."

"Yes. And the problem is, I met him because, well, he was dating my daughter. Real casually. Then we fell in love, and now my daughter won't speak to me."

"And you're surprised?"

"What?"

"And you're surprised she won't speak to you?"

"Well, yes, actually."

"Why?"

"She's my daughter. We've always been real close."

"Do you think you've been a good mother, Gwyn?"

"Yes."

"Does a good mother humiliate her daughter by running off with a guy half her age who happens to be the daughter's boyfriend?"

"Well, I'm not sure."

"Think about it. And while you're at it, look up *slut* in the dictionary."

Dr. Delia cut to a commercial.

I parked my car outside Phil's building. Once again I had an extra lunch. The same fellow who hadn't been home yesterday still wasn't home today. Worrying that he might be dead or in the hospital, I made a mental note to call headquarters so that Wayne or one of the Keiths could investigate. But to me — I must be frank — the fellow was only a name on a manifest, a buzzer that didn't pick up. He didn't signify. He wasn't Phil.

The gate was open this morning on account of some kids who were roller-blading around the pool, so I didn't have to ring. Instead I just walked up the stairs and knocked on Phil's door.

"Surprise," I said when he answered.

"Hey." Phil looked grumpier, more rumpled, than he had yesterday. Had I woken him?

"So I've made your route my route," I said, handing him the lunches.

"That's great." Phil scratched his head. "Sorry if I seem spacey. I was just watching something. You want to come in?"

"Oh, don't worry, I —"

"Come on." And he led me into his apartment. Today the curtains were drawn, which made the living room seem stuffier than it had before. On the television the programming schedule for the afternoon scrolled down against a bright blue backdrop. Lights glowed on the VCR. Had I interrupted him in the middle of a porn video? I wondered, and flushed with worry: after all, the last thing I wanted to do was embarrass him. But Phil didn't seem embarrassed, only tired.

"Listen, can I get you something?" he asked, pulling open a window shade while simultaneously shielding his eyes against the invasive sunlight. "Sorry about the dark. One of the drugs I'm on — I forget which — makes me photosensitive."

"No problem. But you don't have to worry about me. Why not just go back to what you were doing and I'll . . . see you tomorrow, okay?"

"What? I wasn't doing anything. Oh, you mean that." He gestured vaguely toward the TV. "Just an old *Star Trek* episode I've already seen a thousand times."

"Which one?"

"'Is There in Truth No Beauty?'"

"Oh, with Diana Muldaur. I used to watch *Star Trek* all the time when I was in high school."

"So did I. Now I've got the whole series on video. Not that I'm a Trekkie or anything. I mean, I don't go to the conventions, or read those fanzines where Spock goes into Vulcan heat on a desert planet and Kirk has to offer up his butt so he won't die. I just like the show." He smiled a little shyly. "Listen, if it's the end of your route again, you want to watch it with me? We could eat together. After all, there's that extra lunch."

"Oh, I couldn't do that."

"Why not?"

Why not indeed? Certainly no rule in my driver's guide prohibited me from eating with the clients. And yet in all the weeks I'd been delivering for the Angels, I'd never once done so, or been asked to do so. Nor had I ever tasted one of the lunches, even when I had extras left over. Other people did. At the rectory volunteers were forever sticking spoons in pots, licking beaters. Me, I held my nose when I did my bagging. I grafted onto those perfectly good meals the sour smell of hospital trays. I knew who they were being cooked *for.*

Still, I didn't dare explain any of this to Phil.

"I'm not really hungry," I said instead. "But I could sit with you while *you* eat."

"How's about I just put the food on a plate and you do what you want with it?" He went into the kitchen to unbag. "So what have we got here?"

"Roast chicken, sage stuffing, and Key lime pie," I said, taking my place on the sofa.

"Terrific." Phil laid knives, forks, and napkins out on the coffee table, then returning to the kitchen, spooned the chicken and stuffing out of their plastic boxes and onto chipped white plates.

"Well, here you go," he said, sitting down next to me. "Eat hearty."

"*Buon appetito.*"

He aimed the remote control at the television. I recalled only vaguely this *Star Trek* episode, which concerned a creature whose thoughts were among the most sublime in the universe, yet whose physical appearance was so hideous no human could look at him without going mad. Naturally this creature was called a Medusan.

Neither of us was touching his food, I noticed: me for reasons already outlined; Phil, as I later learned, because the Bactrin made him nauseous. Instead we settled into the *Star Trek* episode, which was even stranger than I remembered. The Medusan turned out not merely to be hideous, but "hideously formless." Intermittently he was "shown" — a clatter of staticky sparks, intermixed with psychedelic burblings of color. As for Diana Muldaur, she played a space-age telepathic psychologist who, because she actually *could* look at the Medusan without going insane, was assumed to be superevolved. But as it happened, the reason she could look at the Medusan wasn't that she was so superevolved, it was that she was blind.

Blind! That was the thing that had fascinated me about this episode: not the plot, which choked on its own tail; no, something about the idea of psychic sophistication serving as a front, a convenient ruse by which a person could both mask and profit from a handicap. . . . Julian would have found it interesting. He had this theory that for the vast majority of artists, style existed as a tactic to cover up or circumvent a limitation, an infelicity: to distract the reader's eye from the awkward rhyme, the listener's ear from the dropped note. A theory which, in my case, had great validity.

The episode drew toward its not very surprising conclusion. In the last minutes Mr. Spock established a mind-meld with the Medusan during which the creature said something (through Spock, of course) that I never forgot. "But most of all, the aloneness!" the Medusan said. "You live out your lives in this shell of flesh, self-contained, separate. How lonely you are. How terribly lonely."

After the tape ended, Phil switched off the VCR. For a few minutes we just sat there, in that darkness to which my eyes were starting to become accustomed, staring at the gray glow of the cooling screen. Phil was wearing the same shorts and polo shirt he'd had on yesterday. There was a glitter in his beard. His cutoffs neatly outlined his bundled cock. And yet I couldn't have said whether he was dressed that way to arouse, or for the same reason that sick children wear pajamas all day: because soft cotton soothes sore skin.

It would have been different if I'd met him at the Circus of Books, I thought; if I'd met him anywhere; if I hadn't known he was sick. And I wouldn't have asked. I wasn't one of those people, like Trent, who needed to ask. I'd have taken Phil on faith. Hell, I'd have taken Phil any way he wanted.

Finally I got up. "That was a good one," I said.

Phil disagreed. "Lots of holes in the plot. But I've always liked Diana Muldaur. She was in another episode — I forget the title — where she and Kirk become host bodies for some disembodied brains. And of course Dr. Pulaski on *The Next Generation.*"

"Didn't she also step into an empty elevator shaft on *L.A. Law?*"

"That's right." He smiled up at me. "Listen, I hope you understand if I don't see you to the door. I'm not feeling too great at the moment."

"Can I do anything?"

"I think I'll just sleep. There are good days and bad days, you know?"

"But do you need some milk? I could run out to the supermarket. Do you have any prescriptions to be filled? I could —"

"I'm fine," Phil repeated patiently. "Anyway, Justin — my buddy — he takes care of all that for me."

"Oh, your buddy."

"Yeah."

"Tuesdays and Thursdays."

"That's right. Still, you're nice to offer."

I shrugged. "Okay. Well, see you tomorrow."

"See you tomorrow."

He waved goodbye with the remote control.

As I let myself out I heard the television switching back on.

Now, about the buddy: I would be a liar if I didn't admit that even at this early stage of my friendship with Phil, the knowledge of his presence made me jealous. This was an irrational reaction, of course. After all, I was in no position to make a claim on Phil, or deny him the right to all the help he could get. And yet something about the way the buddy's name kept coming up made me nervous. For that matter, something about his *name* made me nervous: Justin. It sounded like granola and good teeth. Brown ankles. Penny loafers without socks.

In my imagination the buddy blossomed into a nemesis: handsome, young, in better shape than I was; the sort of fellow who would never hang out at the Circus of Books, or talk on phone sex lines, or balk at eating an Angels' lunch. If he were a writer, I decided, he would probably be the kind who worked diligently, getting up at seven every morning so he'd have time to make coffee and take the dog on its walk. Probably he flossed regularly. Probably he owned a Lexus, and listened to Scarlatti, not Dr. Delia, when he drove.

In the world, meanwhile, I was starting to have lunch with Phil every day. Sometimes I even brought him extra goodies, fruit smoothies and whole-wheat fig bars, to supplement his regular meals. This went strictly against policy, as I later learned. In lawsuit-happy L.A., the last thing the Angels wanted was to be held responsible for food poisoning. And yet I knew Phil would never squeal on me. He liked organic fig bars too much — and he liked me. Soon we were openly colluding in defiance of our overseers, with the result that our friendship shed its volunteer-client protocol. Officiality faded into the background. It was understood that even if I quit delivering, I wouldn't quit delivering to Phil.

At that time I didn't have many friends in L.A. Oh, I had plenty of acquaintances — some cousins whose number my mother had given me, my bosses at the production company, men I'd arranged to meet after talking on the phone sex line. With none of these people, however, could I enjoy the easy, uninflected intimacy I shared with Phil. Not that we did much together. Usually we just watched videos; or we talked; or we sat next to each other on the sofa and didn't talk, while outside the drawn shades kids splashed in the swimming pool. This not talking in particular was a new experience for me, since in the past I had always shrunk from silence; indeed, my relationship with Julian might best be described as a nine-and-a-half-year conversation driven by fear, as if to stop talking would be to stop living. But from Phil I was learning that those couples Julian and I had always pitied in restaurants, the ones who didn't say a word to each other, might actually have been happier than we were, might have been not talking not because their marriages had collapsed into stagnation and aridity, but because they had reached that level of comfort and mutual ease that obviates the need for chatter. Or, to invert that famous ACT UP slogan, SILENCE does not necessarily = DEATH; sometimes it = LIFE. Yet so few people seem to know that.

One day when I arrived with lunch he asked me rather sheepishly if I might do him a favor. That afternoon he had his weekly checkup at a nearby AIDS clinic. Usually Justin drove him, but Justin's car had gotten sideswiped on the 101.

"So you want *me* to bring you?" I asked — a little startled, if truth be told.

"Hey, if it's a problem, don't worry," Phil said. "I can take the bus."

"No, no, of course it's not a problem. I'd be delighted. I'd be —" I didn't say thrilled, lest I sound too much like that actress, getting off on her own virtue. And yet my heart raced, my skin flushed. I cringe to admit it, but the prospect of driving Phil to his checkup excited me.

He went into his bedroom; didn't shut the door. Out of the corner of my eye I watched while he shed his polo shirt and cutoffs, threw off his flip-flops, stood naked before the dresser sorting through boxer shorts and T-shirts and wads of white socks. And I thought, Anyone else, anywhere else, this would have been exhibitionism; this would have been seduction. And yet with Phil you could never be sure. It was possible he was giving a show; but it was also possible that his willingness to undress in front of me sprung from an absolute unconsciousness of sexual effect: the nonerotic immodesty of locker rooms.

I turned away, pretended I wasn't looking as he pulled on faded blue boxers, a V-neck T-shirt, jeans and tennis shoes and a rayon shirt patterned with bougainvillea: a really ugly shirt, I thought at first, until I noticed that his chest hair spilled out the collar with the same exuberance as the bougainvillea. Phil had so much chest hair you'd have had to dig for his nipples.

"Okay," he said, coming into the living room. "I'm ready."

"Let's go."

We stepped outside. "Hot today."

"Did you put on sunblock?"

"I forgot. Whoa, that's bright!" Squinting into the light, he felt his pockets for dark glasses.

I unlocked the passenger door.

"This is a nice car," he said, getting in. "What is it, a Pontiac?"

"I think so."

"You think so?"

"I'm not really a car person."

Phil laughed. "You're one of a kind, Jerry. You're the only

person I've ever met who didn't know what kind of car he drove."

"Hey, it's a rental! Anyway, in New York no one has a car. A car is a liability."

I turned the key in the ignition. Immediately Dr. Delia's loud voice boomed out the speakers. "And so we send our kids the message that it's all right to behave in these inappropriate ways —"

I shut her off as we pulled out onto Saturn Street.

"I used to own a Jeep Cherokee like that one," Phil mentioned. "Cobalt blue. I'd only had it six months when I got sick."

"You sold it?"

He nodded.

"Why?"

"Why?" Phil looked at me incredulously. "Because I didn't have any money, that's why."

"I'm sorry. I didn't . . . of course that's why you sold it. I have this bad habit. I talk before I think."

"You don't need to apologize. But anyway, yes, I had to sell it, see, when I came down with PCP, I didn't have health insurance, only life insurance. And suddenly I was looking at, like, fifty thousand bucks in medical expenses. So first I went to one of those, what do you call them, viatical brokerage services, you know, where you can cash in your life insurance if you're terminally ill? But I only got half what the policy was worth. So I work out this payment plan with the hospital. Then just when everything looks like it's going to be okay, like I'm going to be able to dig out after all, this queen in Pacific Palisades I'd done a kitchen for up and sues me. The sink sprung a leak or something. Well, I don't know if you've had much experience with lawyers, but they'll sic the Dobermans on you twice as quick as any car dealer. So it was 'swing low, sweet Cherokee' . . . my beautiful car's swan song."

His voice faded.

"That's lousy, Phil," I said.

"Oh, it's not that bad. I can always take the bus if I need to." He cranked open his window. "Still, there's nothing quite like cruising down La Cienega on a hot day, is there, Jerry? Listening to talk radio. You get hungry, maybe you pull into the Beef Bowl, or have a hot dog at the Hot Dog. You ever been to the Hot Dog? 'Where eight inches is only average.' That's their slogan."

"I'll go this afternoon."

Phil grew quiet. It seemed we were lapsing into one of those easy silences of which in the past I'd been so distrustful. I looked at him: elbow bent in the open window, shirt collar billowing. And I thought, Movement really is his medium. Really, he belongs behind the wheel of a cobalt blue Cherokee, drinking Coke from a huge plastic go-cup as he heads up to — where? Ventura? Lompoc? Some on-the-way place that had never felt like a destination in its life.

And now we were passing a coffee shop straight out of *The Jetsons,* a chunk of L.A. cold war architecture that startled by virtue of its very incongruity: the past's fantasy of the future, grown old. This coffee shop had fins and upthrusts. It had an aerodynamic logo like the emblem on Captain Kirk's chest. It was called Ships, naturally; below the name, the words

NEVER
CLOSED

shrinking away to nothing.

"Ever eaten there?"

"Ships? Sure. I remember when I first came down from San Francisco — this was years ago — we passed it on the way from the airport, and I made George pull over. George was my lover then. Every table had its own toaster, which at the time I thought was pretty cool. I must have been twenty, twenty-two."

"We could go for lunch one day. Maybe on Sunday." The Angels didn't deliver on weekends.

But Phil only shrugged. "The place is sort of sad now. Mostly old men eat there. The waitresses are old. There's even this little disclaimer on the menu, for people who like their food spicy. It says, 'We are salt and pepper cooks.' That always broke my heart, 'We are salt and pepper cooks.'"

"Do you think it's a coincidence, Ships being so close to Saturn Street?"

"It's a good question. To be honest, I never thought about it. But maybe. I mean, L.A. in the fifties was so hung up on this idea of itself as the future. Now all that tomorrow-land stuff's become nostalgia. You know what I'm talking about." And he intoned, "The housewife of the future need never ruin her hands doing dishes! Robots will take care of all those everyday chores, leaving her plenty of time for leisure activities."

"Cars are a thing of the past. The businessman of the future flies to work in his personal shuttlecraft."

"Nuclear-powered monorails have done away with pollution."

"Underground cities leave the surface of the earth an immense park for everyone's enjoyment."

"Vacation time? 'What'll it be this year, honey? Venus?' 'But Jim, we did Venus last year!' 'I want to go to Mars!' 'Hush, Junior! You know we can't afford Mars!' 'But, honey, I just read in the paper, United has a special family rate to Mars, only three thousand monetary units!' 'Hooray! Junior can have his vacation on Mars after all!'"

Phil stopped. I looked at him, amazed.

"Is that real?"

"God knows where it came from. Something stuck in the memory banks. Another one I like is 'Blastermen, activate your scopes.' Have you ever seen —"

The hospital's monstrous facade interrupted him. It filled the viewscreen. Yanking us from space, it pinned our bodies to the earth; demanded obeisance, sacrifice.

I parked in the immense garage. We undid our seat belts, stumbled out of the car into the cool shadowy air. Up we rode in the elevator, up floor after floor to the AIDS clinic, which turned out to be as aggressively cheerful a place as the Angels kitchen, its walls papered with safer sex posters and posters of bright-eyed men and women declaring their HIV positivity and signed headshots of minor celebrities who had once visited, leaving behind these relics so that no one would ever forget they had done a good deed.

We sat down to wait. Across from us a man in a jogging suit was reading *Highlights for Children.* A woman next to him held *Arizona Highways.* Phil was thumbing through an old issue of *Smithsonian.*

I remembered as a kid sitting in dentists' waiting rooms, rifling through stacks of old *Highlights for Children.* I always looked for the "Goofus and Gallant" column, in which the behavior of a very good boy, Gallant, was contrasted with that of his less than polite cousin: "Gallant offers to help Mother with the dishes"; "Goofus leaves the table without saying thank you."

What would have been a modern equivalent? "Gallant

asks, 'Am I hurting you?'" "Goofus says, 'Shut up and take every inch of it, faggot.'"

Needless to say, I'd always had something of a crush on Goofus.

A nurse in street clothes emerged from behind some swinging doors. "Hey, child," the nurse said, rubbing Phil's shoulder. "And where's Mr. Justin today?"

"He got sideswiped. This is Jerry, by the way. Jerry, Lamar."

"Nice to meet you, Jerry." Lamar offered me his long brown hand to shake. "It was very good of you to give Master Featherstone here a lift."

"My pleasure."

"Well, I hope you enjoy our fabulous selection of magazines. In the meantime, Phil, Paula's ready for you."

"Okeydoke." Standing, Phil followed Lamar toward those ominous swinging doors.

"Bye-bye," Lamar said.

"Bye-bye," I said.

"Oh, and by the way, Phil, tell Justin if he still hasn't sold that Soloflex, I might know someone who's interested . . ."

They disappeared. I fell back into my seat. I was thinking of all the waiting rooms I'd languished in during my childhood: most particularly the waiting room of Dr. Craig, our G.P., where I read "Goofus and Gallant" while my mother knit, and in the corner the fish in the fish tank swam from one end to the other; turned around with a single jerk; swam back. There was a diver in that tank, an open buried treasure from which bubbles rose. Probably because I feared needles, even the most mundane visit to Dr. Craig provoked in me that peculiar admixture of fear and boredom for which no quantity of fish tanks or "Goofus and Gallant" columns can serve as antidote. Fear and boredom: it is the odor of waiting rooms. Even now, the accompanying friend, I still smelled it.

Of course, it was worse then. Nurses wore white. Come to think of it, nurses *were* white — and invariably women. In those early days of a stiffer medical establishment, the first sufferers had to endure much more than the disease: they had to endure panic, quarantine, never again seeing a human being who wasn't swathed in masks and booties and rubber gloves. People a generation older than I was all remembered where they'd been when Kennedy was killed: me, I remembered the first time I heard about the disease. I was waiting for the bus that would take me to college. 1979. I bought a newspaper. "Mysterious Cancer Strikes Gay Men in NYC," the headline read; a few nights after which there was a spot on the news. Only queens, it seemed, had this cancer. Flamers. "I don't know how I got it," a sister afflicted with purple lesions told the reporter. "I know I have it, but I don't know how I got it."

Years had passed since then. Today the fear wasn't so much of the unknown as of the overly known: the painful death witnessed a hundred, a thousand times, as if for purposes of preparation, like those puberty movies we'd been shown in junior high school. Of course every effort was made to blunt the edges. The doctors went by first names. Clinics, even hospices, had a tonic atmosphere: so different from that age when nurses wore caps, origami-like, almost mystified in their starched symbolism of folds.

A commotion in the waiting room roused me from this meditation. "I can do it myself!" a familiar voice was declaring, to which the voice of patience responded patiently, "Now just let me help you sit down —"

"I can do it myself, I tell you!"

I looked up. Of course! It was Robert Franklin, clothed now, though still dragging the ornery IV, wearing the orange tennis shoes. The man in the jogging suit turned away. The woman reading *Arizona Highways* turned away. They couldn't help it — and worse, Robert saw that they couldn't help it.

"All right, ladies and gentlemen, just put on your blindfolds. Put the bags over your heads. Forewarned is forearmed. I can do it myself, I tell you!"

Well, in truth there may be no beauty; in truth we're probably all blind telepaths, fooling the world into taking sightlessness for vision. I can't say. I can say only that at that moment, my body felt too small for itself.

I remembered the Medusan; wished, somehow, I could press his words directly into the functional regions of Robert's sorrowing brain.

How lonely we all were. How terribly lonely.

The time line of Phil's life began to ink in for me. He had grown up in a suburb of Boulder, I discovered. His father was in the air force. It was from him that Phil had inherited his fondness for science fiction. But Colonel Pete Featherstone died when his only boy was prepubescent, leaving behind an angry widow, a glut of daughters. Phil waited politely until he turned eighteen, then fled. He bought a bus ticket to every gay boy's mecca, San Francisco. He met Stan. Stan was forty-seven and owned a farm near the Russian River. He invited Phil to live with him. But things didn't work out, and after a few months Phil went back to San Francisco. He met George. George was in his late twenties. They moved together to L.A. Then they broke up. For a while he did "this and that," Phil said; bartended and waitered, clerked in video shops, even got licensed as a masseur — "strictly legit," he hastened to point out. More recently he'd been a personal trainer, and was just making a go of his carpentry business when he found himself dying.

And that, basically, was it. No career, not even any "interests," really, except going to the gym and watching the movies on which his father had raised him. He didn't practice Tae Kwon Do. He didn't make his own pasta. He didn't read biographies of ex-presidents. (To judge from the paucity of books in his apartment, he didn't read anything.) And yet if Phil wasn't a "go-getter," at least he also hadn't wasted his adulthood (as it sometimes seemed to me I had) scrabbling on rat's wheels of ambition and distraction. Instead he lived in the moment, by which I mean that he experienced the moment, he felt the moment on its own terms. Me, if I experienced the moment at all, it was as the anticipated nostalgia of its loss.

Our friendship progressed incrementally. Sex was its asymptote, the arrival it perpetually neared but never reached. At least in my mind. How Phil felt about the matter I couldn't have said for certain. No doubt he must have intuited something of my desire for him. But that desire was part and parcel of its own nullification, namely dread, the ultimate cold shower. It was one of those joke matchsticks that snuffs itself out every time it's lit. It was a self-defeating prophecy. Pulling such mental Rosemarys, I couldn't have seemed a very warm prospect to curl up against in the night. Still, even as I write that sentence, I realize that it presumes something of which I'm not sure: it presumes that Phil might have wanted me in the first place.

Phil worked me up sub rosa. In his presence I never got a hard-on, or experienced a conscious sense of sexual arousal.

And yet when I left his apartment I always drove to the Circus of Books with more impatience than usual; and when I went back to my hotel room afterward, I always found wet patches on the fly of my boxer shorts, as if lust could literally leak out of the body.

I wish I could say I gave up all the bad stuff after I met him, stopped cruising the parking lot and working the phone sex lines and renting the videos. But in fact, in Phil's company my appetite for fast-food sex only increased. I was more on the edge than ever, at the constant mercy of that horniness that crawls on the surface of the skin, never burrowing deep down: all itch.

Julian would have understood this. *Notgeil,* he called what I was enduring: a German word. *Notgeil* was lust with insomnia. It was lust in a hurry. It was waiting room lust, born of anxiety and boredom. And Julian, even more than I, lived in its grip. I used to think he suffered from too many talents. As a teenager he'd played the viola well enough to have a shot at an orchestra post. He painted, oils and watercolors. He sang. He'd had a brief career as an actor, had written plays and newspaper articles. Somehow the very abundance of his gifts panicked him. One by one he unwrapped them, abandoned them. They became simply more toys in that already overcrowded attic where the air was so stuffy, where he found it so difficult to breathe. Soon, from that attic, the only fruition seemed to be *Notgeil.*

I was luckier. I never had to make a choice. In retrospect it occurs to me that Julian, had he decided to, could have outwritten me in a second. But Julian didn't decide to — and my will took me further than his talent. This caused screaming fights on several occasions.

The attic kept getting more crowded. "Everything started never finished," Julian sang from it. Still he wouldn't throw things away. He was a mental pack rat. He lived in a swell of documents, ideas, possibilities; joked that like Leonard Bast, like Alkan, he'd end up being murdered by a bookshelf. Which, more or less, he was.

Nothing started ever finished. But in the end Julian did finish something. The attic burned. Down fell his soul, the madwoman, with hair aflame.

Phil's blood work came back ambiguous. T-cell count down, but just a little. Antibodies up. Such waffly results sounded like good news, to the extent that with AIDS there is ever good news. To "celebrate," I took him out for brunch that Sunday. I made a reservation at a little restaurant on Third Street that the *Weekly* recommended. Phil seemed dubious: egg and bacon places with bossy waitresses were more his speed. Still, he put on his bougainvillea shirt and met me on the curb at the appointed hour.

The restaurant, when we got there, turned out to be a mob scene. There was a reservations desk and an executive chef. The customers were mostly hairless West Hollywood types in muscle shirts. In such a body-waxed atmosphere, hirsute Phil felt his bearishness as an onus, I could tell. Forgoing all the variously sauced complications on offer, he ordered a turkey burger.

Despite the noisiness of the surroundings, I felt tranquil. Usually in restaurants I didn't feel tranquil. I waited impatiently for the food, then when it arrived, ate it fast so I could start waiting impatiently for the bill. In restaurants I shook my leg. I glanced over my shoulder compulsively, as if I were expecting someone. But Phil calmed this frantic impulse. Unlike me, he was never in a hurry except when he needed to be.

Of course, I often asked myself where it had started, this tendency of mine to focus so hard on horizons that I lost sight of the earth rolling away under my feet. The usual suspects appeared in the lineup: Mother, telling me I could be anything I wanted to be, do anything I wanted to do; Father, full of assurances that for such as we, there was no situation that could not be alleviated by pulling strings. Well, Dad learned he was wrong the hard way, when after his second heart attack even the best surgeon in the country couldn't save him; even getting himself bumped up on the transplant list couldn't save him. That someone will always be there to catch you, to bend a rule for you, to finesse you through — it must be the most pernicious of all the pernicious lies that the privileged, meaning only the best, tell their children.

Phil had a different history. He'd grown up with no sense of entitlement whatsoever. To him living in the world was essentially a hostile business, a hot wind you had to fight against. If Phil was stoic in the face of adversity, it was not because he possessed some saintly capacity for patience; it was because his childhood had taught him the essential futility of complaint. He understood that being Hiram Roth's son didn't guarantee you preferential treatment from God.

Acceptance: that was his gift. Not that it was easy for him; indeed, I don't doubt that acceptance takes as much of a toll on the psyche as scrabbling on rat's wheels. Yet at least it is a journey that has an end.

I asked him about his friends. He mentioned Roxy, with whom he worked out at his gym. When he'd first gotten out of the hospital, he said, Roxy had visited him on the average twice a week, but now she was pregnant, and her lover, Dora, didn't want her seeing Phil until the baby was born. "Risk of infection and all that," he added. "I suppose it's understandable."

"Maybe. Anyone else been by?"

"George came last week. He lives in Laguna these days, so he doesn't get into town too often. And Justin, of course." At the mention of Justin's name, he smiled. "Oh, and you, Jerry."

"How about your family?"

"Haven't heard from them lately."

"Do your sisters write?"

He shook his head.

"Yes, but Phil, everyone needs company."

"Company!" He laughed. "That I've had too much of! More company than all the boys in this room combined, I'll bet." He leaned closer. "You know, when I was in the hospital, they asked me if I'd fill out this survey? So I said sure. And I had to answer questions like, How many people did you have sex with in 1981? How many people did you have sex with in 1982? Was your primary sexual activity a) oral, b) anal passive, c) anal active. And I thought about it, and the number of guys I'd had sex with in my life — it was close to three thousand! Three thousand! And I'm thirty-nine. So now George, he's really into these twelve step groups? He calls up one day, and he says, 'Phil, when we were younger, we were classic sexual compulsives. All the symptoms.' Like it's news. And I say, 'Sure, George, but isn't sexual compulsive just a new way of saying we had a good time?' He didn't laugh, though. He takes these things too seriously, George does."

Our food arrived. Looking down at my plate of shredded duck breast, cactus relish, and spaetzle, I envied Phil his turkey burger.

"Does George have a lover now?"

"Oh, sure. Carlos. But they don't have sex. They haven't had sex in like five years, which these days seems to be the definition of lover. So now every couple of weeks George comes into L.A. and picks up a hustler, after which he feels so guilty he calls me up, and goes, 'What am I going to tell Carlos, what am I going to tell Carlos?' And I say, 'Nothing, George. You're going to tell him nothing.' But of course he does tell him, and Carlos goes ballistic, and they have these screaming fights so that the neighbors call the police. Their therapy bills must be through the roof. Anyway, last week George comes by and tells me he's sworn off sex. He says for the sake of his relationship he's moved beyond the need for sex. I mean, maybe I'm crazy, but I just don't get that, Jerry. Because all the relationships I had with lovers, including George, they were *for* sex. Sex was what they were about."

"Oscar Wilde said conversation had to be the basis for any marriage."

"Conversation! I had this one lover from Italy? He could barely speak English! We did great for a year and a half."

"But only a year and a half."

"Well, better a good year and a half than a miserable two decades, if you ask me." Phil played with his french fries. "You probably disagree."

"No! I've just had a different history."

"Yeah? What is your history, Jerry? You know, you've never told me."

He put down his fork, crossed his arms, looked me in the eye. In his steadying gaze he had me cornered. He was right: I'd never mentioned Julian's name in his presence. And why not? Maybe it was all part of my effort to dress in Angel drag, to be the selfless caregiver who didn't impose his own worries.

Maybe I was scared that he'd blame me, as Julian's mother had. Maybe I just didn't want to implicate myself. Another test.

Still, I had to tell him something.

"My history?" I said finally. "Well, I lived with someone nine and a half years. Then he died." I didn't specify how he died.

Conversation halted. Not a comfortable silence this time. I felt that cheap relief you feel when you've gotten away with something devious; and yet the old dread lingered. Having cheated, the fear of being caught lingered. Phil, not Julian, was now the proctor in the exam room of the examined life.

"Jerry," he said, "I hope you don't think —"

All at once a blond boy in a Notre Dame T-shirt and white biking shorts was looming over our table. "Phil, my man!" he crowed, grabbing him by the neck.

Phil, slightly dazed, stood up. "Hey, Kein, how you doing, buddy?" He patted the boy on the shoulder.

"I'm doing great," Kein said. "Did Justin tell you I'm in *Show Boat* over in Simi Valley? A small part, but it's better than waitering."

"That's terrific."

"And you?"

"Oh, holding up, holding up. By the way, this is Jerry. Jerry, Kein."

"Nice to meet you."

"Good to meet you too." Kein turned back to Phil. "By the way, how is Justin these days? I haven't heard from him lately."

"Pretty good. Busy right now."

"Yeah, it's the season. Well, give him my best, will you? And come see me! I can get you comps."

"Sure thing."

"Bye." (This time to me.)

"So long."

He wandered away.

"Friend of Justin's," Phil said.

"Ah, Justin." I lowered my voice. "Listen, do you want to get out of here?"

"*Yes.*"

We paid the bill and left.

"Kein and Justin used to be lovers," Phil explained in the car. "I only met him once. A strange guy. Like, his real name is Kevin Levy. Then he goes and changes it to Kevin Prescott because he thinks it'll be better for his career. Then when all he gets are parts in like *Friday the 13th, Part 978,* he changes it back, and then Justin gets this thing in the mail, a card like a change of address, except it says, 'NEW NAME! NEW AGENT! Kevin Levy is now *Kein* Levy.'"

"Kein! Do you think he knows what it means in German?"

"What?"

"It means 'no.' It means 'none.'"

Phil laughed. "I doubt it. Kein's not exactly what you'd call the intellectual type."

He put his elbow out the window. "I tell you, sometimes it seems like the world's outrunning me. For instance, the other day, I'm thumbing through *Frontiers,* right? And I'm looking at those model and escort ads, when I come across one for this guy who calls himself a 'cuddle buddy.' Cuddle buddy! 'No sex,' the ad says, 'no nudity. Just cuddles. Twenty-five bucks an hour.'" Phil shook his head. "If you ask me, some things shouldn't be sold."

"Cuddle buddy," I repeated.

"Or take these boys at the restaurant. Probably every one of them shaves his chest, shaves his balls. Which is fine. I just can't quite figure it out. Maybe you can tell me. What is the thing about hairlessness? To me they look like Foster's Farms chickens."

"I guess it's an aesthetic. Frankly, I've always preferred hairy men."

"Me too. Which means that these days in L.A., I'm basically shit out of luck. Even the porn videos — you have to get the old ones if you want to see an unshaved, excuse me, asshole. It used to be different. In my day body hair was hot because it was masculine. Even when we dressed up as Lucille Ball, that felt masculine — you know, Lucy Ball with hairy arms. It was like, we knew we were faggots and we liked it. But these guys, with them it's so much about this separate-but-equal thing, about living in the gay neighborhood and eating at the gay restaurant and having *the look,* whatever the look happens to be. I know, I used to go out with some of them, and what I wanted to ask them, I wanted to say, Hey, whatever happened to the sense of spontaneity? Whatever happened to adventure?"

"I guess spontaneity got dangerous."

"Sex got dangerous. It's not the same thing."

We were at a stoplight. I turned and looked at him, his beard phosphorescent in the sunlight.

"I don't know what it means, Phil," I said. "Regression to childhood, maybe. Everyone wants to be daddy's little boy. Or they pack on muscle like it's some sort of armor. To feel protected that way. Or they just rechannel all their energy into working out or biking or volunteering for the Angels. What's obvious is that it's operating from fear. These days everyone operates from fear."

"Maybe," Phil said. "I can't say for sure. I only know that it makes me feel outmoded. Like Saturn Street."

"Saturn Street?"

"Some dead generation's idea of the future, getting yellow around the edges: that's me."

The light changed. We crossed Olympic. On the left, Ships aimed its fins at the stars. I wished we'd gone there instead of the place on Third Street.

We stopped at a video store and rented *Forbidden Planet,* which Phil had been urging me to see. He was just sliding the cassette into the VCR when the phone rang.

"Hello?" he said. "Hi! Yeah, we just got back. No, I can talk." A long pause. "And what did you tell him?"

A smile. A laugh.

"Perfect. By the way, I ran into Kein today." Pause. "The same as ever. Yes. Listen, I'd better go. Yeah. So I'll see you around five, okay? Good deal. Bye. I know. Bye."

He hung up. "Justin," he said, aiming the remote control at the television.

"Oh, Justin," I said.

Forbidden Planet began. I had trouble following its plot, which seemed to borrow heavily both from Freud and *The Tempest.* Early on, however, my ears perked up when one of the astronauts lifted a shiny chrome microphone to his lips and uttered the memorable words, "Blastermen, activate your scopes."

"So that's where you heard it," I said.

"Heard what?"

"That line you quoted on the way to the clinic."

"Oh, yeah. I guess. I didn't remember."

His eyes were fixed on the set. Very lightly I touched him on the shoulder; he tensed; perhaps I left my hand there a fraction of a second too long before taking it away.

Simple as that, I had my answer.

As soon as the movie ended, I got up. "Well, it's nearly three," I said. "I'd better be going."

"What, you're expected somewhere?"

"No, but you're probably tired."

"I'm not tired."

"Even so, you'll want to rest."

"Jerry —"

"You'll want to be fresh when Justin comes."

Phil gazed at me.

"What?"

"Just . . . so you're not tired."

He looked surprised, as if he couldn't quite believe what he was hearing. Then the surprised look gave way to a look of unaccountable sadness. Then he turned away.

"Whatever," he said. Just that: "Whatever." And returned his attention to the blank television screen.

"All right," I said. "Well, see you tomorrow, I guess."

"Sure."

"Bye."

I let myself out.

Back at the hotel I tried to work on my screenplay. But I couldn't concentrate, so I called the phone sex line. Nobody was on it except an old leather queen from Long Beach. Finally around four I got dressed again, went down to the garage, and climbed into my car. For about twenty minutes I drove aimlessly, wishing I could undo things, start again, go back to the real beginning, my very first lunch with Phil. And yet if I could have gone back to that first lunch, what would I have said differently? What would I have done differently? Probably nothing. My fear of illness still would have prevented me from making a move on Phil. And if his behavior today was any clue, Phil wouldn't have wanted me then any more than he did now, either because I was who I was, or because of the illness, or both.

About Justin I still wasn't sure. Yes, that "I know," that "No, I can talk," spoke of intimacy, even trust. But did intimacy mean they were lovers? For that matter, did I really even believe they were lovers? Perhaps I was playacting at suspicion in order to heighten the gratitude I'd feel when at some later date I discovered I was wrong. Or perhaps I wasn't wrong. Perhaps the *real* fake wasn't Phil's affair with Justin so much as my pretending not to believe in it in the first place. In such Rosemarys, and worse, I lost myself for the better part of an hour.

And of course, around five, I found myself turning onto Saturn Street. In retrospect, this seemed predestined. I parked in front of Phil's building. I didn't get out of the car. Some kids on bicycles were chasing a bunch of very black crows that hopped and lunged on the parched lawn. I watched them jump away from the wheels, hop back, jump away again, as if either they enjoyed their own torment, or were too stupid to realize that they could fly away.

A few minutes later a car swung round the corner, a battered white Corolla (I noted the make) that parked directly across from mine. A fellow I judged to be in his late twenties got out. He was carrying a grocery bag. Short, maybe five-seven, with windblown ragged hair, dark eyes, a faint beard. Sinewy and sexy. Locking his car door, he strolled over to Phil's building and rang the buzzer. The gate opened. He went in. It was the last I would see of Justin for a very long time.

I looked at the clock. I told myself I would wait fifteen minutes to see if he had left. But fifteen minutes later he hadn't left. Nor had he left thirty minutes after that.

It started getting darker outside. Switching on the ignition, I drove around the block three times. Each time I returned the Corolla was still there.

At six-thirty the Corolla was still there.

Not anything unusual. Not surprising that a buddy might stick around for an hour and a half.

I went back to the hotel. My jealousy had dissipated, swallowed up by a homesickness so dizzying I nearly swooned. Suddenly I wanted my apartment in New York — our apartment, Julian's and mine. Usually I tried not to think about Julian, for the simple reason that thinking about him made me want to talk to him, which I couldn't do. But now I missed him so much that I did a dangerous thing: I took his picture out from the drawer of the bedside table. I always kept his picture in the drawer of the bedside table because even though I couldn't bear to look at it, I also couldn't bear sleeping without it nearby.

And suddenly, there he was: Julian. Gray-streaked hair, big reddish nose, that weird half smile he affected because he was embarrassed by his teeth. "There's nothing wrong with your teeth," I always told him. But if I have to be honest, like mine, they were slightly yellowed, the result of a wonder drug his mother and my mother and half the mothers of the 1960s had been given during their pregnancies: another outmoded stab at the future.

Nine months, two weeks, and four days had now passed since the afternoon Julian had done away with himself; nine months, one week and two days since the police had found his body, dragging the river . . .

Maudlin emotion flooded me. "Julian," I said to the picture, "oh, Julian, why'd you leave me?" — sounding strange even to myself, like someone in a play, or someone trying to sound like someone in a play. Even where my own emotions were concerned, I had trouble distinguishing the genuine from the counterfeit. I wasn't sure whether this sudden flood of grief was an alias for admitting (as I now had to admit) that I'd fallen in love with Phil, or whether my jealousy where Justin was concerned was a front for pent-up grief, or both. The mask and the face fused to the point of being indistinguishable.

It occurred to me, then, that telling Phil about Julian's suicide might be the trump card I hadn't thought of; the express train to winning his sympathy, even his love. Or would that constitute misuse of Julian's memory? Unfortunately, the only person I could have asked that question was Julian.

I put the photograph away. I redialed the phone sex line. It was busier than before. A fellow called Tim invited me to a jack-off party in Highland Park. Having jotted down his address, I got in the car and drove along freeways and winding hill roads to his house, rang the doorbell, found myself standing face to face with a six-foot-three albino, naked except for two nipple rings and a hoop through his foreskin. And so I turned around, I got back in my car, I drove to the hotel and redialed the phone sex line. Sometimes brutality is the only antidote for sorrow.

But I found no one. You never do in such situations. Even through the telephone, people smell panic. And they run from it.

Around one in the morning there was another botched rendezvous. The fellow, having opened his front door and looked me over, backed away. "I think I've changed my mind," he said.

"No problem," I said.

He shut the door in my face.

I got in the car and switched on the radio. A late-night talk show, the opposite of Dr. Delia. No screeners. The people who called could talk about anything they wanted.

"But if the physical is natural, and the natural is good," a young woman was saying.

"I don't understand your point, Sarah."

"I'm talking about religion. I'm talking about faith. In the body."

"Why do you insist on using these relative terms? What does 'natural' mean? What does 'good' mean?"

"Yes, I agree. I don't know what they mean. And that's why when they say, 'It's not nice to fool Mother Nature,' then what I want to ask is, If the physical is good, why can't we just put two and two together? Love is nature and God is love. Death is nature and God is death. Why can't we connect them?"

I switched off the radio. Not surprisingly, I was back on Saturn Street.

The Corolla was gone.

I kept driving. At the Circus of Books, I rounded up three

videos I'd never seen before and took them all back to the hotel. It was now two-fifteen in the morning. Speeded up, all that ordinary sexual gesturing looked Tourretic, spastic. The liquid flow of fucking became hummingbird flight. Cocks shot into mouths like pistons. Semen flew out in spores. Nonetheless I never took my finger off the fast-forward button. I wanted the world hurried up; a different scale of time.

By three-thirty I was watching the third of the videos. Properly speaking it wasn't a video at all, but rather four late-seventies super-eights strung together and transferred onto tape. A pair of cowboys stripped down, oiled up, on some idealized southern California beach. Handlebar mustaches, flannel shirts. I'd always liked that look.

The movie reached its expected conclusion. A promo followed: highlights from other "videopacs" in the same series, each twenty-minute short reduced to a few seconds for purposes of allurement. The first to be advertised was *Hit the Showers!* Two naked boys, their skin pale because the film had aged, lathered up. The usual. Next came *Working Stiff,* which took place on a construction site. A brawny hand scooped Crisco out of a tub marked "Monkey Grease" . . .

And all at once I lifted my finger from the fast-forward button. Sat up in the bed.

Because in that imaginary construction site behind the screen, in hard hat and overalls, stood Phil: younger, yes; beardless; but Phil indisputably; Phil unquestionably; Phil unbuttoning first one and then another strap of his overalls; then Phil randy and naked, his hard, red-tipped cock pointing straight upward; then — so fast! — Phil fucking another fellow's mouth; turning him over and taking him from behind; arcs of semen spraying, another and another, into the air.

It ended in less than half a minute. Less than half a minute, and this revelation of all the erotic details about which I'd so long speculated — the shape of Phil's erection, the way his face looked when he came — was over. Finished. No secrets left. And I flushed with shame, for I felt sure that from the cloud-cuckoo land of that stage-set construction site, young Phil was watching me as I watched him; me in my hotel bed, naked, the covers pulled up to my waist.

I switched off the VCR. Got up, got dressed, drove to the Circus of Books — not the one in West Hollywood, but the Silver Lake branch, which, like Ships, never closed. Finding the tape in question was easy. No one rented these old films anymore. Phil's picture on the back of the box identified him as Clay Skinner.

Video in hand, I hurried back to the hotel. It was nearly dawn now. I put the cassette into the VCR, fast-forwarded through the shower room, until the construction site materialized. And once again, there he was, in his overalls, his lips moving while he hammered at a wall. No soundtrack: only piano music, like an old silent. But I knew what Phil was saying. He was saying, The housewife of the future. He was saying, Nuclear-powered monorails. He was saying, Blastermen, activate your scopes.

This is not how the story ends, but almost. The next afternoon I found a message waiting for me from the producers of the screenplay I was supposed to be writing. They wanted pages. When I couldn't give them pages, they wanted me. A meeting happened, at the end of which I found myself politely fired. Suddenly I had to pay for the car myself. I had to pay for the hotel room myself.

Unable to afford Los Angeles on those terms, I no longer had a choice. I said goodbye to the Angels; I said goodbye to Phil; I went home.

We kept in touch for a few months: letters, phone calls. Then a long silence, at the end of which a letter in hesitant handwriting arrived. It seemed Phil had suffered another bout of pneumonia; had spent three more weeks in the hospital; was home now, albeit the worse for wear.

Our transcontinental conversation dropped off, as transcontinental conversations tend to do. Each of us had other things on his mind: Phil, the exigencies of an increasingly demanding illness; me, my determination to rebuild a New York life. It was all starting to seem part of a remote past, our friendship, which amazingly enough had lasted only three weeks. I felt my love for Phil ease, release. Not go away. Just become manageable. Something I could package, compartmentalize, store in my own attic, which unlike Julian I was good at keeping tidy.

And then one day, about fifteen months after I'd left, I found myself back in Los Angeles for the most nonprofessional of reasons: one of my L.A. cousins was getting married. Since my father's death, I'd tended to trade off with my sisters the task of escorting our mother to family events, few of which took us so far afield as this one.

Mom and I stayed at a Ramada Inn near Valencia. For those of you who don't know L.A. geography, Valencia is *E.T.* territory, miles from the Hollywood hub where I'd tarried the year before. But I had a rental car, and two afternoons at my disposal. So I called Phil. An answering machine picked up. I left a message that was answered, a few hours later, by another message — this one telling me to call not Phil, but Justin.

Of course my heart clenched when the hotel operator told me that name. I went so pale my mother asked me if I was feeling all right.

I excused myself. I went to my room, where I dialed Justin's number. "Oh, hi," Justin said when I introduced myself. "It's great to hear your voice! Phil's talked so much about you. Listen, thanks for your message. It was lucky I got it. I'd just gone over there to pick up some clothes. He's in the hospital. The pneumonia again, but at least he got through it. In fact he's due to be released this afternoon. And he was thrilled when I told him you were in town. Could you come by tomorrow, say, around lunchtime?"

"Sure," I said. Then, after a second, "Was it bad?"

"It's the third time. For a while it looked . . . well, he made it."

"I can't wait to see him," I said.

"Jerry, I ought to warn you. He doesn't look the way he used to."

"I'd expected that."

"No, but it's really bad. I just want you to be prepared. When you see it happening gradually, you forget. But for people who've been gone . . ."

"I won't give anything away," I said.

"Good," Justin said. "So, he'll be expecting you around midday tomorrow."

"Great."

"Bye."

Simple as that.

I wasn't sure what to bring Phil. Flowers? Candy? Finally I decided to buy him a copy of *Forbidden Planet,* along with a package of the whole-wheat fig bars he'd liked so much.

Around noon I pulled up to his building. Saturn Street hadn't changed much in the intervening months. Oh, the grass was less parched, this being spring. No boys chased crows. Other than that, everything was more or less as it had always been in that sleepy pocket of the future because in my mind memory had not yet shrunken its scale, redrawn the borders. That would come with years.

The gate hung open. As I'd done so many times in the past, I walked around the pool, climbed the cement staircase. The door hung open too.

"Phil?" I called as I knocked.

"Come in."

I went. Phil sat in his usual place on the sofa. Justin had been right to warn me: he was sallow now, so thin the wings of his shoulders protruded through the T-shirt he was wearing. Also, he'd had to shave off his beard. A star map of pimples dotted his chin and cheeks.

"Hello, Jerry," he said, and waved me over to the sofa, where I sat, took his hand, held it to my chest.

"I told you I'd look worse sooner than I'd look better."

"You look good to me."

"Don't lie."

"I'm not lying." I opened the bag I was carrying. "Look, I brought you some organic fig bars."

"Organic fig bars! You know I haven't had those since you left?"

"I figured."

"Thanks. So how's New York treating you?"

"Can't complain."

"The Big Apple. You know I've never been there?"

"You told me."

"Guess I won't get there now." He leaned away. "So did Justin tell you I've been in the hospital?"

"Yup."

"It was a nightmare. I didn't think I'd make it."

"You did, though. You're strong, Phil."

"Maybe I used to be. But this is the last time. Remember you told me once about those lawyers that do living wills? Well, Justin called them up for me. They're sending someone by tomorrow. I'm going to tell them. I don't ever want to be hooked up to one of those respirators again."

I nodded.

"I never got to say how much I enjoyed that time we spent together. I was sorry when you went home."

"I was sorry, too."

"It left a big hole in my day. Jerry, I need —"

Then the bedroom door opened, and Justin walked out. He wore a bright pink and green shirt, white jeans, orange tennis shoes like Robert Franklin's. "Hey, you must be Jerry," he said, striding across the room. "Good to meet you."

"Good to meet you, too."

"You're famous around here, you know that? How great." He shook his head, as if in wonderment at greatness. "So, can I get you something to drink? Dr. Pepper? Pepsi?"

"Just water."

"One water coming up." And he headed for the kitchenette.

Only then did I understand that the thing I'd always suspected was true. And how surprising! The corroboration of what I'd known all along — known, and tried to persuade myself not to believe — felt sadder than any surprise.

"Here's your water."

I looked up. Justin stood over me, just as more than a year ago Phil had stood over me, his shirt falling.

"Thanks," I answered, and took the glass. Drank. Next to me, Phil rubbed his hands together furiously.

"Oh, before I forget, Phil, I brought you something else."

I handed him the videotape.

"Another present! Whoa!" He took it, started to unwrap it. "Hey, a video! Justin, what is it?"

"I didn't know if you actually owned this one —"

"Justin!"

Justin took the video out of Phil's hands, which were shaking. "*Forbidden Planet.* Great! That's always been one of your favorites, hasn't it?"

"Blastermen, activate your scopes," Phil said.

Justin put the video on top of the television.

"Phil's blind, Jerry," he said. "I'm so used to it I forgot to tell you on the phone."

"But I still watch movies!" Phil interjected. "I love the dialogue, the whacked-out music."

"I'm sorry," I said. "If I'd known I would have —" I put down my water glass. I started to cry.

There was another knock on the door.

"Angels," a bright voice called.

"Come in!"

A very young man walked in, fresh-faced, smelling of showers.

"Hey, Dave, how you doing?" Phil said frantically.

"Not too bad. Good to see you again, Phil. I missed you while you were in the hospital. Hello," he added to me.

"Hello," I said, wiping my nose.

"Just put that on the counter," Justin said. "If you don't

mind. So what delicacies have you guys cooked up today?"

"Let's see: cream of mushroom soup, carrot juice, chocolate pudding."

"Sounds great."

"Well, since you've got company, I'll leave you to it. *Hasta mañana.*"

"Bye, Dave!"

"Bye, Dave!"

He let himself out.

I looked at them, then, Phil and Justin. Whatever jealousy I'd felt was gone. It was as if, for the first time, I understood exactly how I'd failed Phil. I'd always been too much the visitor, the hotel dweller, my heart in some other life I refused to talk about. Whereas Justin had made himself resident: in Phil, in Saturn Street. Along with George and Roxy and Kein and all the other people for whom L.A. wasn't some weird, grief-induced dream, but a place to live; a place they had chosen to live.

I didn't know how I'd missed it, Phil's blindness. Perhaps because, like the telepath on *Star Trek,* he'd learned to cover up. Leaving Justin to the task of revelations — a task he dispatched with an almost frightening efficiency.

"So what brings you to town this time?" he asked now. "Doing another screenplay?"

I glanced up. Only then did I notice it, the detail that had clued me into the truth without my even being aware of it. It was his shirt. The bright pinks and greens. I should have recognized that bougainvillea anywhere.

Half an hour later I stumbled back out into Saturn Street. Blinding sunlight. Across from Phil's building, the boy from the Angels sat in his red truck, eating a sandwich and listening to the radio.

"Hey," I said, rapping on the glass.

"Oh, hi!" He switched off Dr. Delia. "You were up at Phil's place, right?"

"Right."

"I'm Dave, by the way."

"Jerry."

Through the half-open window we shook hands. "I just wanted to tell you, you're doing a great thing. I used to work with the Angels myself. That was how I met Phil. I delivered to him."

"Really? You drove this route?"

"A year and a half ago."

"I've only been volunteering a few weeks myself," Dave said. "You know, a lot's changed since you were here. For instance, we're not in that church anymore."

"No?"

"Nope. Now we've got this great new headquarters on La Brea. Plus an executive chef, salaried. Two full-time dieticians. A new managing director from Boston. They did a nationwide search!"

"Managing director! What happened to Sunny Duvall?"

"Sunny who?"

"Not important. And how about the prayer circle? Do you still have the prayer circle?"

"Every morning, though I never join in. Not my scene." He put down his go-cup. "Say, have you eaten? You can have half my sandwich if you want."

"Thanks, that would be nice."

"Hop in."

I did. The cab smelled of dog. Sunlight had warmed the vinyl seats. "I hope you like tuna," Dave said. "I make it myself. My secret is yogurt instead of mayonnaise." He handed me half the sandwich. "So tell me, Jerry, how'd *you* end up delivering for the Angels?"

"A long story," I admitted. "If I tell it right, which up until now I haven't."

"Doesn't bother me. I like long stories."

"You do?"

He nodded.

"Okay. But you'll have to drive. For this one I need to be moving."

Without a word he turned the key in the ignition and pulled out onto Saturn Street.

"Where to, my good man?"

"Anywhere," I said.

"Sounds good to me," Dave said. "I like anywhere. Anywhere's always been my favorite place."